OLIVER
LIT(✓ S0-ARN-409

Queens are Wild

For Angelo

By Jack Chaucer

Copyright 2013 – Second edition

ISBN-13: 978-1484972854

ISBN-10: 1484972856

All rights reserved.

Cover art by Ida Jansson.

Chapter 1

Year(s): Classified
Place: Kingsbury, Nevada

Substitute gym teacher Lou Ventana lowered the volume of the ping on his ST-Warp 5 mobile device and ducked into a utility closet in the bowels of Kingsbury High School. He left the light switch off and focused on the tiny glowing screen in the palm of his calloused left hand.

Sure enough, white letters began to appear on the bright blue screen. Contact was indeed possible with Area 52. Ventana, a 6-foot-3, 240-pound jar head wearing a navy blue windbreaker, black wind pants and black boots, exhaled with relief.

"I take it you arrived in one piece. How was your trip, Lou?" the letters said.

Ventana smiled and used the large fingers on his right hand to nimbly punch his response into the small black keyboard below the blue screen.

"Beyond my wildest imagination," he texted. "Life as a Seal didn't prepare me for that … anyway, I'm fully embedded here. It seems like I've been here a month now, but time is a funny thing."

"Indeed it is," the white letters replied.

"So is it time for the return trip?" Ventana texted.

"Roger that," the letters flashed. "Our window will be open beginning in 72 hours. Use the 8 adjacent rooms on the first floor as A through H. Do U have all your pawns lined up? Our friend 52 is setting up the board, so to speak, for the forward match, if you will."

"Yes," Ventana texted. "The chosen pawn plus 7, mostly bozos who won't be missed. Perfect collateral damage."

"Their sacrifice won't be forgotten," the letters replied. "Password for this game is 'shatranj.' You will be white king. I will direct all moves in coordination with 52, who will control all black pieces for maximum effect and, we hope, minimal risk to our mission target."

Ventana frowned and texted back, "He better let us win. I'm white king after all."

"LOL. Fortunately, 52 claims to be on our side," the device replied.

"He better B. We saved him from a watery grave in '33," Ventana texted.

"Very true. Good luck and Godspeed Lou," the letters flashed.

"Thanks. C U soon. Same 20, different century," Ventana texted before shutting the device off and stuffing it back into the pocket of his windbreaker.

As Ventana slowly exited the utility closet, the faces of the eight white pawns shuffled through his brain.

Chapter 2

Date: March 12, 1984
Place: Kingsbury, Nevada
Seventh-period Spanish class at Kingsbury
High School, located on a sprawling campus just a
few miles from Lake Tahoe, was heaven for the
students and sheer hell for Mrs. Marta Pina, a
former Catholic school teacher who had switched to
the public school system six months ago. With her
tiny stature, humorously broken English and
complete inability to extinguish even the smallest
brushfires of teen rebellion, Mrs. Pina was quickly
overwhelmed day after day by a chair-bound mob
of spoiled punks.

For Margeaux Quigley, a very attractive 17-
year-old senior, A-student and varsity soccer star,
the class was both painful and hilarious to watch.
But her pity for Mrs. Pina certainly didn't prevent
her from looking forward to seventh period every
day. It was like scoring yet another goal against a
hapless opponent en route to an 8-0 rout on the
soccer pitch. Yes, she felt a little bad about it, but

she enjoyed it just the same at the end of another
tedious day of classes.

On this fine March afternoon, it was shaggy
blond-haired Sam Gray -- a habitual offender -- who
rankled Mrs. Pina in the first minute of class by
loudly complaining about the hygiene of Tim
Fields, who sat one aisle over. Overweight with oily
brown hair, a pimply face, poor posture and reeking
of body odor, Fields stood no chance in this class of
mostly bored whiz kids, aggressive jocks and
attention-starved wise asses.

"You're killing me with that stench, Oil
Fields," Sam barked.

Seated toward the back center of the class with
her long black hair pulled back into a pony tail,
Margeaux wore a cream-colored sweater, faded
jeans and blue-and-gold sneakers. Her striking, dark
blue eyes had a perfect vantage point as today's zoo
got under way in this classroom of 32 students -- 19
boys and 13 girls.

Mrs. Pina, a 4-foot-9, 40-something Hispanic
woman with short, wavy brown hair, wore a black-
and-gold checkered long-sleeve shirt and black
pants as she approached Sam with a scowl on her
pouty, petite face.

"Why do you have to be so un-Christian-like to
you friend," Mrs. Pina asked Sam in one of her oft-
repeated laments that had become a punch line all
its own, particularly due to her inability to say the
word "your."

Scattered laughter filled the room as Sam
slumped in his chair under Mrs. Pina's disgusted
glare. The black-and-white sneakers at the end of

Sam's long, jean-clad legs nearly touched Mrs. Pina's short, black heels. Her brown eyes darkened with anger.

"This is not a bar! Straighten up in *you* seat!" the little teacher fumed with both hands flapping to the delight of Margeaux and her classmates.

Yes, comedy hour was just getting started. Seconds later, all eyes and ears rotated 180 degrees as a huge spit ball smacked against the Venetian blinds, covering the top half of a window along the outer wall of the first-floor classroom. That set off another big round of laughter as Mrs. Pina slowly migrated back toward the top center of the classroom.

Pudgy troublemaker Jim Sherman, sporting a buzz cut and black Mötley Crüe T-shirt, smiled so broadly that everyone but Mrs. Pina knew he was the culprit.

As scowling Mrs. Pina walked past the center line of the double-paneled chalkboard, wise ass Scott LaFrance gave a quick hand signal and the laughs died down to complete silence in an instant.

Mrs. Pina paused for a second in the peaceful oasis and decided to try to start teaching.

"Today we will ...," she began, but as she walked back to the right, across the center line, LaFrance looked around with his wild, brown beady eyes, nodded his head and the class erupted into bedlam yet again.

Margeaux giggled. This was a new gag, probably the brain child of LaFrance and his oddball cohorts -- chunky loudmouth Gerry

DiFusco and short, hairy Tommy Sorrentino -- based on the way they spearheaded the commotion.

During the tumult, Margeaux noticed tennis jock Danny Capobianco and his stocky swimmer pal Jimmy Baker under-handing spit balls up to the white ceiling. Two of them stuck there and Danny, who had short curly brown hair and green eyes, flashed Margeaux a flirtatious grin before waving his right hand wildly to get the embattled teacher's attention.

"Mrs. Pina, I'm not sure it's safe to be in this classroom," he said. "Look up at the ceiling."

Mrs. Pina moved back to the left, crossed the center line again and the classroom went silent as she came down the row of desks toward where Danny was sitting, two seats to the left of Margeaux. The teacher frowned, gazed up and attempted to examine what Danny was pointing at -- two wads of spit and paper clinging to the ceiling.

"I'm pretty sure that's asbestos, Mrs. Pina," Danny said, trying to keep a straight face as the class snorted and snickered.

Much to Margeaux's surprise, Mrs. Pina had a rare moment of clarity. She looked back down and scowled at Danny.

"That's terrible," she said, pointing at him. "You get two ceros (that's zeroes in Spanish) for lying!"

"What?" Danny said with his best "who me?" expression followed by a not-so-subtle grin. "That's an outrage, Mrs. Pina. I'm trying to report a school safety issue and you give me two ceros for lying?"

"You also get detention!" Mrs. Pina shouted, stunning Margeaux and her classmates by standing her ground for a change.

Then Margeaux saw why today would be different. The new gym teacher had silently entered through the open door at the front right of the classroom. Clearly he had been eavesdropping on the mayhem from the hallway. The big man with the buzz cut stood there with his huge arms folded across his chiseled chest, which was covered by a white T-shirt. He also wore green camouflage pants and black combat boots. His face was mean and his cold, dark eyes slowly scanned the classroom as if he were taking a mental photograph of every juvenile delinquent in front of him.

Holy shit! Mrs. Pina called in backup. We just might get our asses kicked this time, Margeaux thought.

Then the gym teacher's icy glare stopped and met Margeaux's alarmed blue eyes. Mr. Ventana was his name, she knew, but fortunately she had gym with Miss Stewart. Ventana and Margeaux had never even exchanged glances before, but now this military-looking brute was practically leering at her high cheek bones, ski-slope nose, full lips and sexy, athletic body.

Take a picture freak, it'll last longer. Then again, it might not. He's still staring at me!

"Enough!" Mr. Ventana ordered, finally breaking his glare at Margeaux and silencing the class with one word more effectively than Mrs. Pina could do with 10,000.

The tan-skinned behemoth with the shaved dark hair moved to the head of the class while Mrs. Pina smiled at him and retreated behind her desk at the front left of the room. He spoke with a deep, authoritative voice.

"You people are a disgrace," Ventana thundered, then gestured toward Mrs. Pina. "This woman is trying to teach you something and all you do is show her disrespect and make her life miserable."

All of the students kept silent and hung their heads. Margeaux suddenly felt ashamed of herself for being lumped in with this juvenile manure pile.

"I have observed what has been going on in this classroom for some time and it sickens me," Ventana said with steel in his eyes and a dangerous tone. "All but eight of you will report to after-school detention tomorrow. The eight ringleaders will see me on Saturday at 10 a.m. sharp for a special video presentation designed to reshape your attitudes."

"But what if we can't make it Saturday?" LaFrance whined, knowing he was one of the ringleaders.

"Then you will be suspended and possibly expelled," Ventana shot back.

LaFrance sulked in his chair. Several others shook their heads.

At least I'm not a ringleader, Margeaux thought.

"The eight students who will report to me here on Saturday morning are Sam Gray, Dan Capobianco, Jim Sherman, Scott LaFrance, Gerry

DiFusco, Tom Sorrentino, Jimmy Baker and Margeaux Quigley," Ventana said, staring right at her again.

What the fuck, Margeaux thought. *I didn't do anything and I'm the only girl being singled out?*

"That's bullshit," Margeaux heard herself say out loud, drawing a few chuckles from the class and an "oh no" look from her pal and desk neighbor, Amber Hull. "I was not a ringleader."

Danny smiled at her and said, "Glad you're on our team."

"Shut the hell up, all of you!" Ventana shouted as Mrs. Pina observed it all with a pleased look on her tiny face. Then the jug head fixed his probing eyes back on trembling Margeaux.

"Miss Quigley, you will report on Saturday morning just like the others or you can kiss your soccer scholarship to Stanford University goodbye," he said. "You think you're a true leader, soccer captain? Well, I just watched you sit by, laugh and bat your eyes at all these barnyard animals for the last 15 minutes. Doing nothing about a horrendous situation and passively encouraging it -- where's the leadership there? You better get your head on straight, too, or you'll end up going nowhere like most of these losers!"

Margeaux sat in stunned silence while some of the losers murmured their discontent.

"This class is over," Ventana declared with a vicious scowl. "You don't deserve Mrs. Pina's valuable time and energy. Go home to your mommies and daddies and tell them why you were sent home early today. Tell them they've got a lot

11

of work to do before you're ready to enter the real world. You better get started right away. The clock is ticking toward graduation -- if you graduate."

Margeaux and her classmates quickly stood up and scrambled out of the classroom under Mr. Ventana's unblinking glare.

...

"I have Saturday detention," Margeaux declared two minutes into a scrumptious dinner of roast chicken, cheesy scalloped potatoes and green beans.

Margeaux's doting mother, a fit but drained single mom of two who appeared older than her 45 years, stopped chewing and looked puzzled. Margeaux's younger brother, Michael, a tall, gangly 15-year-old with braces and a brown-haired mullet, reveled in the news. After all, he was traditionally the troublemaker in the family. He grinned ear to ear as he gobbled on a drumstick.

"Sweet," he said with his mouth full of food.

"How on Earth did you get Saturday detention?" her mother asked with a pained expression and disappointed blue eyes. She had short brown hair that was graying and wore a lavender sweater as they sat at the dining room table of their modest one-level ranch house in Kingsbury.

"Spanish class is a zoo because the teacher is incompetent and we all got in trouble, but it's totally ridiculous that I was the only girl who got singled out -- seven boys and me got Saturday detention," Margeaux said before taking a drink of lemonade.

"What did you do that the teacher got so upset?" Michael asked with excited hazel eyes.

"Well, let's see, I believe I laughed, yeah, that's about it," Margeaux said bitterly. "The boys in the class raise hell, throw spit balls, disrespect Mrs. Pina and I get punished for giggling. I can't help it -- sometimes it's funny."

"Well done, sis," Michael said, trying to give her a high-five, but Margeaux frowned and left him hanging. "Margeaux, you're really one of the boys now."

Her mother just shook her head and tried to eat some potatoes, but tears welled up in her eyes. She was visibly shaken that her overachieving daughter suddenly regressed, potentially starting a pattern of behavior that could jeopardize her senior year and a full-ride to Stanford.

"Mom, will you please chill out and say something?" Margeaux finally pleaded.

"I don't know what to say," her mother replied. "I just think it sets a terrible example for your brother."

"Yeah," Michael concurred with a chuckle. "My brain is buzzing with ideas to top big sis as we speak!"

"Shut up!" Margeaux scolded him.

Their mother just shook her head again. Margeaux felt ashamed, frustrated and angry. She needed to kick something. She got up, quickly tied her hair into a ponytail, cleared her dishes off the table and set them in the dishwasher. Then she grabbed two white-and-black soccer balls out of her red duffel bag on the kitchen floor and headed out the back door.

Margeaux pictured Mr. Ventana's face on the balls as she blasted them again and again into the backyard net.

Chapter 3

Date: March 15, 1984

Place: Kingsbury, Nevada

Margeaux parked her gold Chevy Malibu sedan in the largely desolate Kingsbury High School parking lot, situated to the left of the main building on a flat, semi-circular campus ringed by small trees and shrubs. The sun was climbing into a beautiful blue sky -- absolutely the wrong kind of day to be locked up in Saturday detention. Margeaux got out of her car and noticed some of her fellow soon-to-be inmates loitering in front of the two-tier brick building's main entrance.

Danny Capobianco sped through the parking lot in his red Iroc-Z sports car blasting the new Van Halen hit "Jump." He parked diagonally across two spaces next to Margeaux's car. He often did that when the lot was full, too.

What a dick. At least he's hot, Margeaux thought.

Danny, wearing a black T-shirt, blue jeans and neon-orange tennis shoes, slammed the car door and quickly caught up with Margeaux as she walked toward the school. The two had a history of flirting but nothing more. Perhaps the bonding experience of Saturday detention would set the stage for a senior prom date. He was a little too cocky and flashy for Margeaux's taste, but she wasn't wowed by any other potential prom candidates either. Prom was still two months away. She would leave her options open for now and see who emerged.

Though she didn't have a boyfriend at the moment, Margeaux knew she was attractive enough to get one whenever she desired. All she had to do was convince herself that a particular boy was worthy of her attention and affection. That was the hard part. There was no point in getting into a serious relationship now anyway. Soon she would be heading to California for college -- assuming she could stay out of further trouble.

"The only positive thing about this detention is you got stuck with us, too, Margeaux," Danny said, smiling and turning up the charm as he strolled alongside her. The other six boys congregated near the double doors, talking, spitting and laughing.

"Thanks for the compliment, but this sucks," Margeaux replied with a wry grin.

"Yeah, especially on an awesome Saturday like this," he said.

Then, at exactly 10 a.m., rugged jar head Mr. Ventana pushed open one of the double doors and ushered the gang of eight inside.

"Good morning," he said, dressed in a tight, gray short-sleeve shirt, green camouflage pants and black high-top combat boots. "Come right in."

Margeaux and the boys filed quietly behind Mr. Ventana and down the locker-lined hallway toward a first-floor classroom on the left.

"I'll brief you in here," Ventana said, studying each of their faces as he held the door open and waved them through with a burly left arm.

Brief us? What is this, police headquarters? The Pentagon? This guy is such a tool, Margeaux thought.

The gang of eight sat in a semi-circle of chairs set up near the front of the classroom as Mr. Ventana walked to the teacher's desk and began sorting through stuff in a big navy blue duffel bag.

Margeaux sat next to Danny and felt the eyes of the other six boys sneaking looks at her -- smart ass Scott LaFrance with his thin build, short dark hair, mischievous eyes, long nose and pointy chin; Gerry DiFusco, overweight and boisterous with a jolly face and close-cropped black hair; portly Jim Sherman, who had a light-haired buzz cut, brown eyes, round face and a trouble-making perma-grin on his fat lips; short, brown-haired Tom Sorrentino, who wore glasses and had a wiry, wrestler's physique; tall and lean Sam Gray with his furtive blue eyes, playful smile and wild blond hair; and Jimmy Baker, the avid swimmer with short reddish-brown hair, freckles and a penchant for saying things like "Call me Bake" and "That's the Baker way."

When Mr. Ventana retrieved a bunch of items from the duffel bag and handed them out to the gang of eight, Jimmy Baker surprised everyone by immediately responding with enthusiasm.

"A swim cap -- awesome," Baker said, hoisting the orange cap for all to see. His reaction made sense, of course, because he was a member of the varsity swim team. "Are we hitting the pool?"

Mr. Ventana just glared at him and he shut up quickly.

Margeaux and the other boys were more interested in what looked like a hand-held computer game.

"Turn it on like this," Ventana told the group as he showed them where the power button was on the side of the little black gadget with the blue screen and small black-and-white keyboard.

As they all followed his instructions, their blue screens glowed brightly and the boys erupted in excitement.

"Now hit your G buttons twice," Ventana instructed.

Margeaux and the boys followed orders.

"Space Invaders!" Jim Sherman shouted with delight about the popular 1980s video game. "How did you get it on something so small? I'm used to playing it at the arcade."

"So cool!" Danny, Scott and the others agreed as they began playing with the gadget.

Margeaux, meanwhile, ignored the game and inspected the other two items Ventana had handed them. The biggest one was a weird orange zip-down vest made of heavy material that seemed to match the orange swim cap. The cap itself was bizarre, too. It felt bumpy, with small nodules covering every inch or so.

What the hell is this guy up to? Margeaux feared.

"See, Saturday detention isn't so bad," Danny declared as he started rapid-firing at virtual aliens.

Ventana allowed himself a small, eerie grin at that -- a facial gesture that literally sent shivers through Margeaux's already-tense body.

"I'm out of here," she heard herself say as she stood up in the semi-circle.

The seven boys seemed confused and annoyed at being distracted from their games.

"Sit down Miss Quigley," Ventana said firmly but calmly.

"What is the purpose of all this? A video game? A swim cap? A strange vest?" she asked, feeling a little faint as she stood there awkwardly. "These boys may be getting a kick out of this, but I'm not. Something is not right about this and I don't want to be any part of it."

"Whoa, chill out," Danny told her, putting his hand on her arm. She bristled and pulled her arm away.

"What is going on here?" Margeaux repeated. "We deserve to know the truth."

Ventana folded his huge arms across his massive chest and finally began to provide an explanation.

"First, sit down, Miss Quigley," he said, his dark eyes boring into her until she complied. "Second, boys stop playing your games for a minute and I will tell you all what will happen from here."

The boys stopped playing after a few moments and looked up at the large man.

"Now you will all take your games and equipment I gave you and go into eight separate classrooms to the left of this one down the hall. Each room has a letter taped to the door. Enter the classroom with the letter that corresponds to the small white letter on the back of your game."

Sure enough, there was a small white "C" on the back of Margeaux's game.

"Once inside your designated classroom, I will give you further instructions," Ventana told the group, which listened closely to every word.

"Is it going to be a Space Invaders contest -- like highest score gets to leave detention first?" LaFrance asked with a hopeful tone.

"Yes, something like that -- only you might learn something along the way," Ventana said with shifty eyes.

He's lying to our faces. He's telling us 2 percent of what the fuck is happening here. This is some kind of scientific experiment, shock therapy or something. I just know it, Margeaux thought.

Margeaux recalled a scene from the Stanley Kubrick movie "A Clockwork Orange" she had seen without her mother's permission a couple of years ago. Amber Hull's older brother had rented it and they watched it during a sleepover. Margeaux remembered how they had strapped the lead character to a chair, pried his eyelids open and forced him to watch a bunch of films. They altered him so he felt sick any time he wanted to have sex or hurt people, and then he went crazy.

"Take your things and go!" Ventana ordered, snapping Margeaux out of her daze and flipping on her panic switch.

No explanation? Nothing!?!

"But," was all she managed to mumble.

"Now!" Ventana shouted over her and pointed toward the door.

Margeaux trembled, but she fought back the tears. She didn't want to give this meathead the satisfaction of seeing her cry. She could be tough. She could kick some ass. She stood up, aggressively grabbed her video game, swim cap and vest, and followed the seven boys out the door.

Ventana watched them enter the rooms marked A through H and then followed them down the hall.

When Margeaux entered the "C" classroom and heard the door being locked quickly behind her, she immediately dropped her equipment, wheeled around and lost it.

"Fuck you, asshole!" she shouted, banging her fists on the door. "I'm gonna call the police on your ass if I ever get out of here!"

Ventana, as if he knew how she was going to react, stood there gazing at her through the door's thick glass window for a moment with a creepy "gotcha" expression on his face.

Margeaux froze, realizing all eight of them were now completely at the mercy of this mysterious and possibly dangerous control freak. She shrank back from the door and closed her eyes to break his stare. When she re-opened her eyes, Ventana was gone. She could hear his black boots walking down the hall to lock Rooms D through H.

She wanted to scream to classmates, but nothing came out.

Margeaux glanced around at the classroom and freaked out even more. All of the chairs and the teacher's desk had been removed. She eyed the windows and rushed to try to open one of them, but when her fingers grabbed the latch, she recoiled in agony from the stinging shock and fell to the floor. Now tears were filling her eyes.

What the hell? He put an electric fence around us?

"Get up off the floor, Miss Quigley," she heard Ventana command, but his voice was coming from the video game she had dropped on the floor back across the room. She scrambled over to it, picked it up and saw Ventana's face staring back at her on the 3-by-5-inch monitor. She had never seen anything like it obviously -- it was 1984, not an episode of "Star Trek." Then she looked at the little buttons below Ventana's image -- they said A through H and K. She pushed A. In a flash, Jimmy Baker was staring back at her.

"Hello Margeaux, it's Bake," he said with a big grin and the orange swim cap already covering his round head.

"Take that thing off. You're a fool. Wake up!" she yelled at his image before cutting off his attempt at a reply and punching the B button. She saw Danny's handsome face and long eyelashes. For a second, she felt a pang of relief until he said, "Hey, you're interrupting my Space Invaders. I'm blasting …," he said, before Margeaux cut him off with a shrill diatribe.

"He's got us penned up like sheep surrounded by an electric force field and you're at the fucking arcade! Get us out of here you useless douche bag!" she screamed at him.

"Relax Margeaux, you're so paranoid. Don't you know paranoia is the first sign of an alcoholic?" Danny's image wisecracked at her. "These picture phones are so cool. I ..."

"Screw you, too!" Margeaux shouted before pushing the C button and erasing his image. Her own screen lit up in blue and Space Invaders was ready to start. She flipped off the screen with her middle finger. Then she pushed buttons D through H so fast that she saw the faces of the other five idiots flash before her eyes, but she couldn't remember what order they were in and, frankly, didn't care. While fighting through sobs, she punched the K button, and once again was greeted by the smug face of her captor, Mr. Ventana.

"Hello again, Miss Quigley," he said with a satisfied grin. "Shall we get started?"

"I demand ... demand an explanation!" she shouted at him.

"Put on your swim cap and vest and you'll get one," he said flatly. "This helpful video program will improve your leadership skills, patience and respect for authority."

"My ass it will," she seethed. "This isn't authority. This is kidnapping!"

Chapter 4

Year(s): Classified
Place: Kingsbury, Nevada

"Miss Quigley and all the rest of you, please put on your swim caps and vests now so we can get started with this program," Mr. Ventana's face commanded on the little blue video screen that Margeaux held in her left palm. She was amazed at how clear and light the device was, but she tried to maintain her focus. She sensed in her gut that Ventana was going to do something horribly wrong to them, but the seven boys didn't seem fazed at all. They were going along with the program every step of the way and even seemed to be enjoying it.

Is it just me? Am I paranoid? I'm sure as hell not an alcoholic, as Danny pointed out. Then again, I definitely could use a stiff drink to calm my nerves right about now.

"Fine," Margeaux said, setting the device on the floor, putting her hair in a bun and reluctantly donning the strange orange swim cap and matching vest. "But if I ever get out of here, I will call the police on your ass, Ventana."

24

Saying that made her feel slightly better, but Ventana simply ignored her and continued on.

He's so infuriating!

"Good," was all he said when he saw that she had put on the cap and vest. He checked in on the seven boys as well and made sure all eight of his captives were in compliance. Margeaux wondered what room Ventana was in.

"Now everyone punch the letter associated with your room," Ventana ordered with a blank expression on his face as Margeaux picked up the device again and held it in her right palm this time.

Again, Margeaux felt the urge to challenge him, but this time she decided against it. She already had made a fool of herself in front of Danny and the others. And now she was actually curious to see what would happen next. This was quickly turning into the strangest Saturday of her short life. Little did she know, the most bizarre events hadn't even happened yet. She pressed the C button.

As soon as all eight students had hit their assigned buttons, Margeaux's room began to vibrate like there was a minor earthquake shaking the building. She gripped her mobile device tightly and looked around the room. The distant trees outside the window stood still, she observed, but the room was definitely shaking.

Then the vibrations grew much stronger and the chalkboard in front of her began to disappear into a fog! Seconds later, the fog turned bright and Margeaux's body seemed to float upward into white nothingness -- no walls, ceiling, windows, trees, chalkboard or floor. She felt light as a feather and twirled in what appeared to be a zero-gravity void. The vibrations still sounded strong, but now she could not feel them with any part of her body.

"What the ...?" she thought.

Margeaux allowed herself to turn upside down, perform a few swim strokes and tumble around. It actually felt free and liberating. She almost forgot she was a captive for a moment.

Then Ventana's face reappeared on her little black gadget with the blue screen. She gazed back at him with a very different expression on her face -- a bit of whimsy. He observed that change in her and gave her a pleasant smile for the first time. Suddenly, Ventana didn't look like a domineering brute.

"Now you know why I waited to give you an explanation, Miss Quigley," he said. "This is not so easy to explain."

"No, I can see that," Margeaux said with a slight grin as she rolled in zero gravity. "Are you turning us into astronauts or something?"

"Not exactly," Ventana said as the rumbling in Margeaux's white room quieted down to more of a steady hum.

"Any other information would be greatly appreciated," Margeaux prodded him, but this time with a softer tone.

"Now that we've reached a comfortable cruising position, so to speak, I will tell you that we are about to engage you in a special game of chess," Ventana told the divided-up gang of eight on their futuristic gizmos. "That is why half of you are in white rooms and half of you are in black rooms."

Margeaux hit the B button on her tiny keyboard and, sure enough, Danny grinned at her wearing his orange swim cap and vest, illuminated only by his little screen's image of her, against a black backdrop.

"What a pretty flashlight you are," Danny said, still cocky and charming as ever despite the most bizarre detention in the history of education.

"What the hell is going on, Danny?" she asked him.

"No clue, but it ain't boring at least -- I mean this zero-gravity shit is amazing," he said.

Ventana's face reappeared on Margeaux's screen -- apparently he had the ability to override their interactions -- and he asked them, "Are you all familiar with chess?"

"Yes," Margeaux said, though she hadn't played in a few years. She used to beat her younger brother Michael all the time and he would fling the pieces around in frustration.

"Very good," Ventana said, getting affirmative replies from the entire group.

"You will move forward as situations present themselves," he continued cryptically, "and attack when appropriate."

"Excuse me?" Margeaux asked in disbelief.

"Your smart phone doubles as a sword while your vest acts as armor during an attack or as a life preserver in the event you encounter a rook surrounded by a moat," Ventana explained. "Also, your swim cap will keep your brains from exploding, so never, I repeat never, take it off. Understood?"

What the fuck?!! Margeaux's brief oasis of calm was over and her heart raced again. Ventana kept a perfect poker face as he, too, donned his swim cap and vest on the little blue screen. *Is this guy some kind of sick-fuck male stewardess giving us safety instructions before the flight to hell?*

"No, definitely not understood!" Margeaux shouted at the jar head on her *"smart phone???"*

Ventana ignored her again.

I crave the chance to kill this guy, Margeaux fumed in her swim-capped brain.

"The world is not flat, the universe is not flat and neither is this chess board," Ventana droned on. "Opportunities to move, attack or be attacked will come from all sides, above, below and diagonally. Be alert at all times and do your best. Some of you may not see much action at first or for quite some time -- that is the nature of the game -- but stay ready and good luck. We appreciate your participation. This game should last approximately 52 minutes for those who have watches, though it may seem much less for some and much more for others."

Why does it feel like he's looking right at me when he says "much more?" Margeaux thought, then glanced at her slim, purple wrist watch and noted the time was 10:27 a.m.

"Am I going to have to fight somebody? Is that what you're telling me asshole?" she yelled at Ventana's face, but his image disappeared without a response and Margeaux trembled as she struggled to right herself in the white zero-gravity nothingness.

She clutched the little phone in her right hand and wished it had 9-1-1 buttons.

It doubles as a sword?!! What the hell is he talking about? None of this makes any sense whatsoever. Margeaux whipped the device around like she was preparing to duel, but it felt so light and she could see no blade at all. *Probably because Ventana's lying again. He wants us to think we've got a weapon in our hand when we've actually got squat!*

Margeaux felt like a sucker with zero control. *This must be what it's like for Mrs. Pina when she's trying to teach us. At least she gets a paycheck. I'm getting kidnapped for free!*

Then another thought occurred to Margeaux as she pictured her brother Michael hurling chess pieces across the dining room table.

"Chess, he says, and there are exactly eight of us," Margeaux scoffed out loud to no one in particular. "We're literally a bunch of pawns!"

Chapter 5

Year(s): Classified
Place: Kingsbury, Nevada

"This is my chance to be a Jedi," Star Wars enthusiast Sam Gray told himself as he squeezed his smart phone/sword with his right hand and prepared for battle in the black Room H.

Strands of Sam's stringy blond hair snuck out the back of his orange swim cap as his normally laid-back blue eyes scanned the room nervously, trying to anticipate what would happen next. He had zipped up the orange life vest over a black T-shirt. The zero gravity flipped him upside down and suddenly he could see his blue jeans, white socks and black-and-white high-top sneakers above him as the smart phone's blue screen lit up in the darkness. The beautiful face of Margeaux Quigley stared back at him. She was visibly agitated in a white room.

"We are the eight pawns, so look out!" she shouted at him before disappearing just as quickly.

"What?" Sam asked out loud over the low, steady hum all around him. There was no answer.

He hit the C button on the phone that had illuminated when Margeaux spoke, but nothing happened. Perhaps she was warning the other "pawns" in rapid succession. But he was the H -- he was the last. It didn't make sense.

Neither did the sudden earthquake all around him -- a force so surprisingly strong that he lost his grip on the smart phone and couldn't regain it when the mounting surge of energy behind him pushed him forward upside down with blinding speed. He catapulted out of darkness, through a white room for what seemed like 10 seconds and back into a black room just as quickly.

"Holy shit," Sam screamed, especially terrified by the fact he left his "sword" two squares back. "What the fuck is going on? I don't remember dropping acid last night!"

Sam managed to get himself righted in the zero gravity and tried singing the ACDC song "Back in Black" to calm himself, but then a white door opened several feet diagonally above his left shoulder and a black-hooded assassin burst through. Sam tried to move away, but he just spun in place like a trapped bug with all four limbs flailing as the ninja rushed toward him with a silver dagger. Just as the blade was about to slice into Sam's long, soft, white neck, his brain fried like an egg inside his swim-capped skull.

...

Gerry DiFusco was better at inflicting damage with his mouth than anything else. He loved to crack jokes, bust balls and laugh the loudest. His booming voice was his best offense and defense in a world where he was considered fat; in truth, he was short and plump like a bowling ball. But right now, all his loud mouth could produce was blubbering and crying in the white Room G. Margeaux's warning on his smart phone only had served to ratchet up his agony.

Not even the refreshingly foreign sensation of feeling light as a feather in zero gravity could cool the burning fear coursing through Gerry's meaty head and body, which were already constrained by the too-tight cap and vest. He could have passed for an orange in a Fruit of the Loom underwear commercial, but this orange kept tumbling over like a rotisserie chicken on an invisible spit.

"Get me out of here!" Gerry screamed as he kept pushing various letters on the smart phone with his sausage-like fingers. Faces of his classmates came and went -- swim cap after swim cap -- and his panic level soared even higher.

But when the earthquake rumbled and the surge of energy launched him from white room through black room and back to white again, Gerry summoned something inside him. An adopted child never wanted by his real mother, he tapped into that innate anger of rejection and whipped his "sword" around with such force that he beheaded an invading ninja before he knew he was about to be attacked. What a lucky stroke!

"Take that asshole!" Gerry shouted as he watched the black pawn's dismembered head and body plummet into white nothingness and disappear below him.

"Did anybody see that? I just killed something!" Gerry howled with delight as he started punching the letters on his phone again.

"I can't see shit Gerry, I'm in the dark," Tommy Sorrentino's hairy face and nasally voice squawked from the phone. "What's happening?"

"I just killed a black pawn, Tommy!" Gerry bellowed with pride. "It was fucking awesome!"

"That's great Gerry," Tommy replied. "I'm just floating here in the dark. I can't see nothing, even with my glasses, and I'm so hungry I could eat the balls off a mouse. Plus my head is itchy from wearing this fucking swim cap!"

"You bitch too much, Tommy," Gerry told his friend before hitting his own G letter to unburden his ears and brace himself for the next attacker.

He didn't have to wait long. An L-shaped passage way opened up before his frightened black eyes, the white turned to black all around him, the sound of hooves pulsed through his ears and a black knight in black armor crashed a black sword into Gerry's thick head so fast he never had a chance to raise his arm. Gerry's eyeballs singed from the jolt and his mouth never made another sound.

. . .

Margeaux checked her watch again. It was 10:35 a.m. -- eight minutes that had seemed to drag on forever. She was still floating and tumbling around in her white Room C waiting for action and fearing the worst. She had checked in on Danny a second time and he, too, was doing nothing in the black Room B. After warning the other six boys they were pawns in this mysterious game, she didn't bother checking in on them again. She no longer wanted to know their fate. It would only make her fear unbearable. It was all she could do not to give in to convulsions of crying at this very moment.

Then Margeaux felt the tremors begin and a surge of energy behind her, but she went nowhere and it stopped just as quickly. She twirled around in zero gravity and saw nothing had changed -- until she heard Ventana's penetrating voice. He was not visible and her phone was not illuminated with his face, but the jar head's unmistakable voice could be heard behind her.

"Miss Quigley, I'm in the square behind you," Ventana said. "I just castled. Do you know what that means?"

"Uh … yes. I understand what castling means on a chessboard asshole! Not while wearing a swim cap in zero gravity for Saturday detention!" she shouted with a totally flustered voice into the white nothingness. "Could you tell me what castling has to do with changing my bad attitude and improving my leadership skills? Do you realize I'm extremely close to dying of a heart attack? Does that get through to your thick skull at all?"

"I won't let you die," Ventana told her confidently.

"That's why you're castling behind me, not in front of this poor helpless pawn. Thanks a lot, coward!" she shouted, punching her clenched left fist at nothing.

Ventana's voice laughed. Margeaux had never heard the brute laugh before. Oddly, it made her relax for half a second. It reminded her of a laugh she had heard as a young child -- her father's laugh. She missed that memory of him terribly. He had left her mother when she was only 4 and her brother was 2. He had a new family now, and Margeaux ripped him for it every time she saw him or spoke to him. She hadn't seen her dad in person in at least three years -- *another invisible coward.* Margeaux fumed again at the equally invisible Ventana.

"What are you going to do with me -- a 17-year-old girl?" she screamed. "This isn't fair. I deserve a full explanation!"

"You certainly do," Ventana's voice replied with a rare hint of empathy. "Miss Quigley, you are the reason for this mission."

Margeaux shook her head. "Why am I just floating around and doing nothing then?" she asked.

"Once all of our pieces are in place, you will be the most important pawn on the board and you will move forward with lightning speed -- trust me," Ventana said. "Enjoy the stillness while you can."

"Who are you really and where are you taking me?" Margeaux pleaded.

"You will know in 40 minutes," Ventana said.

Margeaux checked her watch. 10:39 a.m. Then she stopped asking questions and steeled her blue eyes for the unknown.

Chapter 6

Year(s): Classified
Place: Kingsbury, Nevada

Tommy Sorrentino was a heck of a wrestler at 142 pounds, but he knew it would be hard to pull off a takedown in zero gravity. His other forte was complaining -- and this was the perfect opportunity to do a lot of that. He rapid-fire cursed so much that he was more likely to say motherfucker between words than take a breath.

"These mother-fucking bastards better let me the fuck out of this mother-fucking place before I rip this mother-fucking swim cap off. I don't care anymore. I'll mother-fucking explode my brains all over Room F -- got that, mother-fucking Ventana?!" the bespectacled Sorrentino shouted as he jammed his hairy, monkey-like thumb on button K again and again. There was no response from the detention master, which, of course, prompted a new vicious cycle of curses.

Sorrentino had good reason to be cracking up. Unlike some of the other pawns, he had jumped

36

forward three squares already -- from black to white, again to black and then to white again. He knew chess well. He sensed he was dangling out there like a fish head in front of a shark, and there was plenty of chum in the water. The swim cap gnawed at his itchy, hairy head and mocked him. "Go ahead, take the mother-fucking thing off. End it already!" he could hear it say.

And yet, Tommy couldn't bring himself to do it. He thought Ventana sounded a little too believable when he said his brain would explode if he ripped off the cap. He was still giving the detention master the benefit of the doubt.

But when the black bishop appeared above him from out of nowhere -- veiled face, puffed-up black hat and a string of black beads in his right hand -- Tommy only had time to scream one motherfucker before the beads encircled his neck, imploded his brain and put him out of his mother-fucking misery.

...

Jim Sherman had ridden the wave of energy forward from white Room E three times, felt the zero-gravity effect switch off suddenly and got dumped into a fast-rising pool of water. He was now sobbing and bobbing in the dark -- with water bubbling up to his double chin. He couldn't swim, so the life vest Ventana issued him was the only thing keeping him afloat. Lightning snaked far above him, briefly exposing a black castle looming hundreds of feet over his head. The dreaded moat Ventana had hinted at earlier now flooded the black void so fast Jim barely had time to piss his pants before he was nearly submerged.

"Help!" was all Sherman could muster in between gasps as the water lapped over his mouth. His sword/phone was long gone, lost in the scramble against the fast-rising water. It wouldn't have helped in this ominous scenario anyway.

"Help!" Jim yelled again as he splashed and flailed.

Then a bolt of lightning zapped the surface of the moat like a spitball smacking into a Venetian blind -- and Sherman's brain got rooked.

...

Scott LaFrance, left to rot in the blackness of Room D since the whole nightmare began, was not comfortable in passive mode. He liked to take control, surge to the front and set the pace when he ran the 1,600-meter race in track. He also liked to be the first one to make the girls laugh in a classroom or social setting.

But on this particular Saturday morning, LaFrance was stuck in neutral, chafing in his vest and swim cap. He was tired of tumbling in zero gravity and had flung his sword/phone away in frustration.

When the veiled black queen finally arrived to reap the grim LaFrance, she opened a door from what seemed like a mile in front of him and let a tiny ray of light strike his wary eyes. A second later, she stood in front of him and skewered him between the eyes, her long, thin blade dividing his head like the line of demarcation on a two-paneled chalk board. His brain lobes -- left and right -- both sizzled quietly.

...

At 10:44 a.m., Margeaux Quigley felt a massive surge of energy behind her and finally blasted forward into the blackness. As she did, she looked straight ahead at what appeared to be a movie screen and observed images of herself. She saw Danny Capobianco dancing with her at what looked like the senior prom. She had her black hair in an elegant up-do and wore a gorgeous red evening gown with a high sexy, slit up the left leg -- a dress that likely didn't meet her mother's approval. She moved nimbly in long, fancy red heels as Danny, wearing a black tux and red cummerbund to match, twirled her around and dipped her. Then they kissed and smiled at each other.

Soon the images began to shuffle before her eyes much faster. She saw herself scoring a goal for Stanford University and being mobbed by teammates on a soccer pitch. She watched herself walking across a huge stage dressed in cap and gown and then accepting a diploma. She observed herself wearing a navy blue power suit and addressing the jury in a courtroom. And finally, she was speaking at a podium in front of supporters with signs.

That's when Margeaux blasted forward again -- into a white room. She could hear Danny's voice, but the images on the screen were too pale against the whiteness all around her.

Seconds later, she surged forward into the black and there he was -- Danny Capobianco on the movie screen as clear as day. He looked more handsome and much older -- early 30s perhaps. He wore a sharp, dark gray business suit and snazzy red tie. He was talking on a small cordless phone and sitting at a desk in an office building. There was another building visible in the window behind him. Margeaux's stomach churned with pangs of love and tremors of fear as she watched him.

The camera moved backward, away from Capobianco and out a different window. The movie seemed so real as the camera raced back and upward to reveal two skyscrapers -- the World Trade Center in New York City. Margeaux had seen the towers before in person when her mother had taken her and Michael on a Big Apple summer vacation a few years ago. They saw a musical called the "The Fantastiks" and took a ferry ride to the Statue of Liberty. The twin skyscrapers watched over them like two concerned parents as they traveled to and from Ellis Island that day in 1981.

The camera suddenly stopped moving as it loomed above the skyscrapers and Margeaux watched in horror as a jet plane came out of nowhere and smashed into the very tower where Danny Capobianco had just been talking on the phone. Fire balls and debris exploded against the clear blue sky.

"Oh my God no!" Margeaux screamed. "Danny! What is happening? Is this real? Ventana? Talk to me!"

There was no response. Then another jet slammed into the second tower. Margeaux burst into tears as the movie screen seemed to shift into fast forward mode. One tower fell. The other tower -- the one with Danny inside it -- also crumbled into dust. Death and destruction everywhere. Margeaux shook her head and sobbed as she watched the images flash before her eyes. She wanted to peel the swim cap off and die, but Ventana interrupted her agony. His face appeared on her smart phone.

"Margeaux, look at me please," he said.

She did and the movie screen went dark, matching the blackness all around her. The only light in the room now came from Ventana's face on the little blue screen.

"About Danny," he said with a serious expression on his face and a surprisingly sensitive tone. "He was supposed to reach our destination, too. We didn't realize until moments ago that that would be impossible."

"Really? Will you stop talking to me like I know what the hell is going on and level with me for a change?" Margeaux pleaded.

"Danny died in the terrorist attacks on the World Trade Center in New York in the year 2001," Ventana told her in the softest tone he could muster. "His original person could not make the journey beyond that year so neither could any other version of him survive."

41

"Thanks, what is this, 'Buck Rogers and the 25th Century now?'" Margeaux said bitterly as she tearfully punched the letter B on her smart phone again and again to no avail. It remained stuck on Ventana's square-jawed face. "I show up for Saturday detention, you kidnap me to the future and kill off all my classmates for good measure. Thanks."

Ventana let Margeaux have the last word this time. Her blue screen went dark and she surged forward again into white bewilderment.

Chapter 7

Date: October 14, 2035

Place: Aboard the Chinese aircraft carrier "Invincible" in the Pacific Ocean

"Tell the prime minister we're getting all our sharks in a row to give Old Glory a makeover -- all in black," Robert Ballentine told the Chinese interpreter next to him in a meeting of a dozen men inside a long, narrow conference room aboard the ship. They sat at an oak table that nearly ran the length of the room and drank afternoon tea as the sun, shining through two rectangular windows, ducked in and out of the clouds every few minutes or so.

Ballentine, dressed in a sharp black suit with his salt-and-pepper hair pulled back into a ponytail and a well-kempt mustache and goatee, certainly had the look of a corporate pirate, if not the real thing. A 51-year-old oil, shipping and media magnate in both Australia and America, the extremely wealthy Ballentine was nearly ready to go throttle up with his ultimate conquest. What better way to spend your golden years than as king?

For now, the incurably ambitious Ballentine would have to settle for ruling the second most powerful nation on Earth -- China had surpassed the United States in the 2020s.

The world's top superpower certainly liked the jingle of Ballentine's deep pockets. The hopeful monarch was prepared to give China an advance of $500 billion toward paying down America's massive trade debt in return for extensive covert military and high-tech support in coordinating the coup and securing the transition of power.

In addition to Ballentine, the Chinese prime minister and an interpreter, the top secret meeting was attended by a Chinese admiral and general; a Chinese high-tech expert; Ballentine's security chief Andre Belanger, and five representatives of the various turncoat sleeper cells within the U.S. government that would help make the coup possible. The plan was to paralyze the executive and legislative branches of the federal government (not the judicial branch; Ballentine saw it as weak and useless); shut down all major media outlets and utilize his own media network for propaganda during the transition of power; infiltrate and disrupt the U.S. military leadership; and, if possible, take the president hostage to ward off major counterattacks.

In 2035, America was wobbly and weak from decades of debt, and extremely divided both politically and socio-economically. Though the nation's first female president was doing her best, no one person could right America's sinking ship anytime soon. Bottom line, there was no better time to strike than right now for Robert Ballentine. He had the wealth, resources and connections to attempt it. To put it more crudely, he also had the balls. "Balls," after all, had been his nickname since college, where he streaked naked across the football field during the Texas-Texas A&M football game in 2006. He later graduated from the University of Texas at Austin.

Born on January 1, 1984, in Melbourne, Australia, Ballentine smiled from ear to ear as he thought about what present he'd like to get himself for his 52nd birthday.

"Tell the prime minister we'd like to make our move on New Year's Day," Ballentine told the interpreter.

The small Chinese man with the thick dark glasses, short black hair and charcoal-colored suit listened to the interpreter and nodded emphatically. Then he told the translator something.

"Prime Minister Cho asks will it be American New Year or Chinese New Year?" the young Chinese man told Ballentine.

"American," Ballentine said. "We'll let the ball drop, so to speak, in Times Square and then Balls will pounce -- right when they're all good and piss drunk -- about 12:02 a.m. on New Year's Day."

Balls laughed loudly, as did the normally stoic Belanger and the five turncoat liaisons. Most of the Chinese men smiled and nodded politely when they got the translation, but the prime minister remained a bit more reserved. Then he talked to the interpreter for almost a minute.

"Prime Minister Cho approves of the plan," the translator finally told Ballentine, "but he says you are the key to this agreement. Your life is our insurance. If you are killed in the attempted coup or transition of power, China keeps the $500 billion, withdraws all covert support and claims to have had no role in this plot. North Korean mercenaries will be used in the overthrow. We will blame them and you, a United States-educated terrorist, for attempting this regime change."

Ballentine smiled broadly, admiring the Chinese leader's deft, pre-emptive spin-doctoring. Then he leaned toward the prime minister and stared into the bespectacled face of the most powerful little man in the world without blinking his icy blue eyes.

"Always bet on black, mate," Balls said.

Chapter 8

Date: March 16, 1984
Place: Kingsbury, Nevada
Fernando Pina brought the front section of the Sunday newspaper into the bedroom and held it up for his wife to see.

"Marta, you better read this. You might've taught these kids," said the short man with the kind brown eyes and neatly cropped graying mustache and beard.

Mrs. Pina rubbed the sleep out of her eyes, propped up the yellow pillow behind her small back and held out her right hand.

"Let me see," she said, reaching for her eye glasses on the nightstand with her left hand and putting the newspaper on her blanket-covered lap.

The big bold headline said, "FIVE FALLEN KNIGHTS," referring to Kingsbury High School's nickname. The smaller headline below it said, "Kingsbury students found dead under mysterious circumstances, police say."

"Dios Mio!" Mrs. Pina gasped as she saw the mug shots of the dead students -- her Spanish students, the same ones who had enjoyed tormenting her day after day in seventh period since September of 1983. Their angelic faces, suddenly silenced forever, now stared back at her -- Scott LaFrance, James Sherman, Sam Gray, Gerald DiFusco and Thomas Sorrentino. Tears flowed out of Mrs. Pina's eyes and down her cheeks even though she had seen their demonic sides.

"I did teach them … I tried anyway … they were so horrible to me," she said, sobbing. Fernando put a hand on his wife's shoulder as he sat next to her in bed. He knew she had struggled with the switch from private to public school. The higher salary had come at a cost -- too much stress for his little wife of 22 years.

"They're in a better place now … or perhaps not, based on what you've told me about them," Fernando said.

Mrs. Pina certainly didn't believe they deserved death. She shook her head, reading the story with tears in her eyes and a tissue in her hand:

KINGSBURY, Nev. -- Eight students -- all wearing swim caps, life vests and in possession of small cordless phones not manufactured anywhere in the world in 1984 -- were found in separate classrooms at Kingsbury High School on Saturday night. Five are dead, three survived and their Saturday detention monitor -- Louis Ventana -- is missing, police say.

Nevada State Police Lt. David Miller said a custodian discovered all eight students non-responsive in eight separate first-floor classrooms, all of which were locked.

"Five individuals were deceased, but there were no visible signs of foul play," Miller said.

The dead, all seniors from Kingsbury, are Scott LaFrance, 17; Thomas Sorrentino, 17; James Sherman, 18; Gerald DiFusco, 17, and Samuel Gray, 17. Autopsies will be scheduled this week to determine the cause of death. A memorial service for all five students will be planned in the coming days, school officials said. Grief counselors will be available at the school beginning Monday morning. Classes are canceled until further notice, officials said.

The three surviving students, all seniors from Kingsbury, are Margeaux Quigley, 17; Daniel Capobianco, 18, and James Baker, 17. They were treated and released from Kingsbury Hospital on Saturday night and will be questioned by police after they've spent time recovering with their families, Miller said.

"The surviving students had passed out and had virtually no memory of what happened to them other than reporting for Saturday detention," Miller said. "We will talk to them again as the investigation continues."

Authorities, including the FBI, are actively looking for Louis Ventana, Miller said. Though he was identified as a gym teacher and discipline specialist by a school department source, Ventana's address and background were not made available Saturday night.

"We'd like to question Mr. Ventana," Miller said, describing him as a 6-foot-3, 240-pound Caucasian with a muscular build and military-style haircut and clothing.

When asked if the students had fallen victim to some kind of cult activity, Miller said, "We're not ruling anything out at this point. This is already the strangest case I've ever been involved with, and we've only just begun to probe it."

Mrs. Pina sobbed and slumped over into her husband's embrace.

"Maybe it's all my fault. I trusted them with Lou and … and … Dios mio," she mumbled as she wept on Fernando's shoulders.

…

Mrs. Pina and her husband attended the memorial service for her five deceased students at St. Jude Church. The individual funerals would come after that. Not only did Mrs. Pina have to endure nasty looks from parents, friends and relatives of the dead students, but she also had to sit through a sermon and five eulogies praising each student for his wonderful qualities, unselfishness, unforgettable smile, love of learning, etc.

Mrs. Pina knew the truth -- that all five were spoiled, disrespectful punks -- but she bit her tongue, frowned in silence and prayed for their wretched little souls anyway.

Outside the tall, long and narrow church, Marta and Fernando Pina practically bumped into Margeaux Quigley, her sullen mother and bored younger brother Michael.

"Sorry," Mrs. Pina said, suddenly confronted by another withering look from a protective mother.

Margeaux, wearing a black dress and heels with her dark hair pulled back tightly into a ponytail, motioned Mrs. Pina over toward an open area to the left of the pack of mourners filtering out of the service. She wanted to nip the awkward encounter in the bud before her mother said anything. She also wanted to apologize.

"I'm the one who is sorry, Mrs. Pina," Margeaux said with sad blue eyes. "We treated you so badly in Spanish class. I personally feel awful.

"Maybe we ... they ... deserved this," Margeaux added, nodding toward the church in reference to the "Five Fallen Knights."

"No, no, no," Mrs. Pina told her, relieved over Margeaux's apology and embracing her student warmly. Margeaux towered over her, especially in long black heels. "Nobody deserves to die. They were bad kids, but maybe they would've gotten better -- who knows? Now they won't ever have the chance. It's a shame and I feel just terrible."

"Me, too," Margeaux said with watery eyes. "I wish I could remember what happened on Saturday. It's so frustrating not knowing -- not being able to help the police. I talked to Danny and Jimmy, and they don't remember anything either."

"Don't worry Margeaux," Mrs. Pina said, clasping her student's right hand with both of hers.

OLIVER WOLCOTT LIBRARY
LITCHFIELD, CONN.

"Mr. Ventana tricked me, but they will find him and the truth will come out. It always does."

Margeaux shook her head, looked the little Hispanic lady in her droopy brown eyes and felt sure about two things.

"No, I have a feeling Mr. Ventana is long gone and hard to find," she said. "And I'm pretty sure there's a part of me that's gone, too."

...

Two days later, Mrs. Pina was rolling her shopping cart past the paper towels and toward the rack of newspapers beyond the end of an aisle at the local supermarket. A tabloid headline caught her eye.

"STUDENTS ABDUCTED BY ALIENS AT NEVADA SCHOOL," the words screamed out to her.

Mrs. Pina left the cart on the side of the aisle and went to grab the small paper. She turned inside to the article and read it:

KINGSBURY, Nev. – The five students who were found dead last Saturday at Kingsbury High School in Nevada died of electrocution from specially equipped swim caps that they wore during what was supposed to be detention, autopsy reports reveal.

Sources close to the investigation say the five also wore life vests with zippers that doubled as dog tags.

"There were very small engravings on each zipper that were only readable with a magnifying glass," according to a source close to the investigation. "They each identified the victim by name and as having died bravely in the service of the United States. But the real baffling thing was it gave the date of March 15, 2036. That's 52 years in the future."

Equally puzzling, authorities say, is why the three surviving students have no memory of what happened during that Saturday detention session with their still at-large instructor, Louis Ventana.

But physics professor Dr. Mark Sumner of the University of Nevada-Las Vegas offered a theory.

"There's a real chance these students were contacted by aliens or some form of higher intelligence from the future," Sumner said, noting the bizarre, high-tech cordless phones they had in their possession. The FBI has forwarded all of the equipment to its crime lab in Virginia for testing.

"The big mystery is why those eight students were selected -- and why five died and three lived? We've already got Area 51 in east Nevada. Now it looks like we better make room for Area 52 on the west side of the state."

Mrs. Pina put the paper back on the rack and shook her head. She felt dizzy, closed her eyes, opened them again after a few seconds and slowly exited the market. She abandoned her cart, half-filled with groceries, right where she left it -- in Aisle 5.

Chapter 9

Year(s): Classified
Place: Kingsbury, Nevada

At 11:15 a.m., Margeaux Quigley felt the surge of energy behind her again and blasted out of a white room and into blackness. She gripped her phone/sword tightly ready to strike, but once again there was no adversary. She was beginning to believe Ventana's pledge that she would not be harmed, that she was the reason for this whole insane situation.

Once the surge subsided and her heartbeat settled down to match the low, steady rumble all around her, the giant movie screen came to life again. She saw a woman with shoulder-length gray hair, blue eyes and a sharp navy blue power suit waving to a large crowd. There were blue-and-white signs everywhere that said "Quigley-Vaughn 2032" and "Go Margeaux Go" and even "Girl Power."

The woman joined hands with a tall, thin black man with short, graying hair, glasses, a warm smile and a dark brown suit. The crowd went wild as they waved together on the stage and confetti began snowing all around them.

Margeaux focused on the woman's face, read the signs again and laughed out loud in disbelief.

"Are you trying to tell me that I'm going to be president or something?" she shouted, then punched the K button on her phone.

Ventana wasn't answering. He hadn't responded in quite some time. She was frustrated, but not enough to dampen her excitement over the life-like images flashing before her in the dark.

Could this be true? Why else would they be going through all this trouble if I weren't somebody important? I must be president. But why are they bringing me -- a teenage version of that woman -- into the future?

She had no sooner thought of that question when the beginnings of an answer began horrifyingly playing out before her transfixed eyes. She observed the older version of herself standing next to a tall man with a tuxedo, short gray hair, bright green eyes and rugged good looks. They were attending a formal party with plenty of VIP guests. Everyone was gazing at a gigantic TV screen -- the ball was about to drop in New York's Times Square.

"10, 9, 8," they all counted, holding hands with their dates. "7, 6, 5, 4 ..."

Margeaux's stomach roiled with dread. It was like she knew what was coming before it happened.

"3, 2, 1 ... Happy New Year!" the people shouted, cheered, hugged and kissed.

Margeaux began to cry as she saw her older self kiss her handsome date. She had never seen him

before in her life. Clearly, the two were in love --
the president and the first gentleman, she deduced.

As 'Auld Lang Syne' blared in the elegant
ballroom, several people dressed in black with black
hoods that covered all but their sinister eyes
infiltrated the room and began shooting with small
pistols. Margeaux saw herself take a bullet in the
right leg at close range and fall to the floor. Her date
punched out the assassin before he fired a second
shot, but another black-clad assassin pumped
Margeaux's date full of bullets and he fell on top of
her. Other important people also were being shot
while some guests were just beginning to realize
what was happening.

Four men in dark suits with guns finally
converged on Margeaux and her date. Two men
hoisted them up while the other two provided cover.
They all rushed out a nearby door, leaving behind
bursts of gunfire, terrifying screams, overturned
tables, and broken glasses and plates. The movie
screen went dark and matched the blackness all
around her. Margeaux shivered in fear and touched
her left leg. It felt fine.

*It's all just a nightmare. It can't be real. I'm
17. I fell asleep in detention. I'll wake up soon,* she
thought.

"La, la, la … wake up already!" Margeaux
screamed in the dark. She punched the K button.
Nothing. Then she went backward -- H, G, F, E and
D. Nothing!! She was C. She couldn't bring herself
to punch the letter B. That was Danny. She already
had witnessed his terrible fate. Then she punched
the A button.

Just like that, there was a small blue light in the darkness and the orange swim-capped face of Jimmy Baker appeared like a grinning beacon of hope amid the gloom.

"Yo Margeaux, what's up? It's Bake," Jimmy said, like everything was hunky-dory. "I'm still floating around in limbo here. What a waste of a cap and vest. I'd much rather be swimming laps right about now. What's going on with you?"

Where to begin? I'm president. I just got assassinated, yet here I am -- still alive and talking to you, a kid I never said two words to in Spanish class. Other than that, everything is completely as it should be.

Nevertheless, Margeaux smiled with relief that she wasn't completely alone.

"Not much," she deadpanned. "And you, Jimmy?"

"Call me Bake," the apparently unflappable and always personable Jimmy Baker told her.

"OK, Bake, have you had a chance to swim in a moat and battle a rook yet?" she asked, happy to be distracted from her presidency for the moment and play teen again.

"Nope, this is so boring except for the zero gravity effect," Bake said with earnest blue eyes and a pudgy, freckled and friendly face. "I asked Captain Lou what my mission was and he just told me to be patient. He's keeping me in a defensive posture, whatever the hell that means."

Margeaux allowed herself to chuckle. She realized she could do a lot worse than be trapped in a time warp with this kid. He certainly was an upgrade over talking to Ventana.

"I've been doing nothing for like 50 minutes -- what gives?" asked Bake, who clearly loved to hear himself talk and was thrilled to have beautiful Margeaux as his chat buddy.

Margeaux checked her watch with the light of the smart phone. Pretty close. It was 11:18 a.m.

"Then this should all be over in like a minute or less," Margeaux told him.

Bake laughed.

"Yeah, that's what Captain Lou told us -- 52 minutes or less. Like we can believe anything that knucklehead tells us," Bake said.

"He's been right about a lot more than I gave him credit for so far," Margeaux heard herself say as the fear and frustration tugged at her insides again.

"I just hope it's over fast," Bake said. "I'm so hungry I could die."

And I might be dead already, Margeaux feared.

Chapter 10

Date: December 31, 2035
Place: Reno, Nevada

Jimmy Baker prepared to ring in the New Year sharing a bottle of cheap champagne with his much younger colleague, Wendy Lowell, an attractive website reporter with a drawl that greeted you like a "Welcome Oklahoma" sign on a flat, lonely highway.

Bake, as he still preferred to be called, had graduated from the University of Missouri in 1988 with a degree in journalism and worked at a newspaper in San Jose, Calif., before coming to the Reno Gazette in 2006. He had been there ever since, working as a sports reporter, news reporter and digital information manager when the newspaper ceased print production in 2022 and switched to a website-only format.

Bake had seen the staff shrink from nearly 80 when he started to its current paltry total of six. He and Wendy, the youngest member of the staff at 24, had drawn the short straws and were stuck with the New Year's Eve shift.

Now 68, Bake should've been retired by now. But the Social Security program ended in 2029 because of a lack of funds and he had never been much of a saver. He still felt young at heart and kept in decent shape as an avid swimmer, but he also enjoyed his vices -- chewing tobacco, gambling in Reno and Las Vegas casinos, and drinking at local taverns. He also never married, preferring the thrill of the chase over settling down to the point where he was too old and set in his ways to be marriage material.

Working the New Year's Eve shift with Wendy -- each quaffing coffee cups of champagne as they scanned their tablet computers, typed on their virtual keyboards and posted local, regional and national news stories to the website -- reminded Bake that he still had it pretty good compared to most of the country. The rich had gotten much richer, the poor were starving and criminally desperate, and things looked bleak for just about everybody in between. At least Bake still had a job and a paycheck -- even if it was only enough to afford a one-bedroom apartment in Reno. Many Americans could only dream of having their own apartment. More and more homeless roamed the streets on foot or lived out of their undersized hydro-electric cars -- if they could still afford the price of fuel cells.

Bake and Wendy sat in cubicles across from one another in the spacious, mostly empty and underused newsroom. They watched the large flat-screen TV monitor craning over them. It was anchored to a thick beige pillar that helped support the run-down, two-story building. CNN's coverage of the ball drop in New York City blared down on them as Bake and Wendy joined in the countdown to 2036.

"20, 19, 18 …," Bake shouted, his enthusiasm drawing a warm smile from Wendy, who had shoulder-length brown hair, chocolate brown eyes, a small nose, thin lips and cute dimples. She was 5-foot-5, slender and wore a maroon sweater, blue jeans and brown, furry boots. Bake, as usual, wore his black-and-gold University of Missouri cap over his balding, pudgy head, a gray-hooded sweatshirt, blue jeans and white sneakers.

"17, 16, 15 …," Wendy counted, getting up from her chair and joining Bake, who was now standing under the elevated TV monitor.

"14, 13, 12, 11 …," Bake said, hugging the young reporter and grinning like a teenager.

"10, 9, 8, 7, 6 …," they counted together as they pushed together their coffee cups, smiled and downed champagne.

"5, 4, 3, 2, 1 … Happy New Year!," they shouted together as they watched the ball drop in Times Square and then shared a hearty embrace.

"C'mon, give old Bake a kiss," he said with a chuckle, pushing his luck.

"Oh, all right you dirty ol' man," Wendy said. "I'll give y'all a kiss."

She planted a juicy one right on Bake's red cheek. He beamed and blushed like a school boy.

"Oh yes, now I can die a happy Bake," he said, and they both laughed.

Then they returned to their cubicles to resume working. It was only 10 p.m. their time after all, but they always treated the Times Square ball drop as the official new year kickoff. All the subsequent time zones seemed anticlimactic after that.

A few minutes later, Wendy noticed something on her tablet computer screen that made her cry, "Oh my God!" Then she covered her mouth with her left hand and looked stunned.

"Wendy, what's the matter?" Bake asked after having taken a short walk to the water fountain and back.

"This year is off to a horrible start -- look at this news alert," Wendy said before covering her mouth again. Bake came around to her cubicle and looked over her shoulder.

"The president was shot at a New Year's Eve party in Arlington, Virginia, just after midnight EST. Her condition is unknown at this time. Updates will follow," Bake slowly read the words out loud in disbelief, then reacted with flapping arms. "Holy shit! What a buzz kill!"

"I can't believe this, can y'all -- and on New Year's Eve?" Wendy said. "What is this world coming to?"

Then they heard CNN quickly switching gears on the TV monitor above them.

"We interrupt our New Year's Eve coverage to bring you an alarming news bulletin. CNN has learned that President Margeaux Quigley, First Gentleman Bradley Cyr and numerous others have been shot in what appears to be a highly coordinated attack on the highest members of our federal government."

"This can't be happening," Wendy burst out, practically in tears. Bake shook his head, frowned silently at the TV screen and hugged his co-worker, in a much more fatherly way this time.

The CNN female news anchor, clearly frazzled and not completely prepared to come on the air with the story of the century just after midnight on New Year's Eve, paused for a moment, listened to the voice in her earpiece, fumbled for words and then continued.

"We now have word that Vice President Leonard Vaughn also has been shot at a separate event in the Washington D.C. area," she said. "No word on his condition or the president's condition at this time. President Margeaux Quigley, age 68, who is running for re-election this year, was shot at a formal New Year's Eve party in Arlington, Virginia. Unfortunately, details are limited at this time."

Bake and Wendy, locked arm in arm, stood dumbfounded for a moment.

"Who the hell is running the country now?" Wendy asked.

"Speaker of the House, but I wouldn't want to be in his shoes right now, I'll tell you that," Bake said before shuffling back to his tablet computer. "I gotta start posting this stuff to our website."

"Oh yeah," Wendy said, springing back to action. "I'll post some photos of Quigley and Vaughn up there, too."

The CNN coverage droned on above them as they returned to work.

"Correspondent Chuck Dennis is on the line via his iWatch (an Apple-made watch, first introduced in 2025, that doubles as a small voice-activated phone with camera for Skyping and monitor for watching TV or movies)," the anchor woman said. "Chuck, what can you tell us?"

"I'm two blocks from the Sheraton Hotel in Arlington, Virginia, where President Quigley was shot just minutes ago, but that's as close as I can get -- the streets are blocked off and ...," Dennis reported before the TV monitor zapped off and the Gazette's newsroom lights went out.

"Holy shit!" Wendy screamed in the dark. "I did not drink enough champagne to prepare myself for a night like this!"

"This is friggin' crazy!" Bake agreed from his chair in the dark.

Their two small computers were the only illuminated objects in the newsroom until the building's generator kicked on after a short delay and all the lights came back on. Seconds later, regular power was restored. However, Bake and Wendy quickly noticed CNN did not come back on the TV screen.

Instead, there was a black screen with bursts of white letters scrolling across every few seconds that read, "CNN has lost power, the USA has lost power, the transition of power has begun, stay tuned for a new era in this great land, stay tuned for regime change."

"OK y'all, where's that champagne bottle?" Wendy asked with an exasperated expression and both hands up in the air.

"On my desk," Bake said, leaning over the cubicle divider and handing it to her quickly.

Wendy took a long slug directly from the bottle and passed it back to Bake, who did the same.

"I mean could this be some sick April Fool's joke a few months early?" she asked.

"No, I don't think this is a hoax," Bake said with a grave face and a serious tone, not something Wendy was used to seeing from him. "I was alive in 2001, you weren't, and this is starting to feel a lot like that, maybe even worse. These guys, whoever they are, are actually controlling the media directly. That's a whole new twist," Bake said, picking up a remote and attempting to change channels on the TV. They saw the same black screen with white letters on every channel. "This is not well. This is a hard scene."

"Well, when my grandkids ask me some day where I was on New Year's 2036, I can tell them I was with Bake in the Reno Gazette newsroom," Wendy said, trying to lighten the mood.

It worked. Bake's loud, personable presence filled the room again. His smile made her feel better, too.

"When your grandkids ask you that, raise a glass for me will ya, Wendy, because I'll be swimming laps somewhere in the great beyond," Bake said with a chuckle before tucking some tobacco inside his lower lip.

"I shall, Bake, I shall," Wendy said, "if any of us live through tonight, that is."

Seconds later, the black screen with white scrawl was replaced by a red screen with a solid black flag. Underneath, in all white letters, it said, "United Kingdom of America," and classical music played, apparently heralding the aforementioned regime change.

Moments after that, a stout, white middle-aged man with a dark ponytail, graying mustache and goatee, and black suit faced the camera while leaning against the front of a huge oak desk. His arms were folded across his large chest and he stared at Bake, Wendy and the rest of America with bubbly blue eyes and an arrogant smile. There was a solid black flag hanging on the wall over his right shoulder.

"We've been taken over by an actual pirate, for God's sake," Bake shouted at the TV.

"Look at this guy!" Wendy chimed in as they converged under the monitor again and hushed each other when the pirate began to speak. They hung on every word as his deep, ready-for-radio voice alternately alarmed and soothed them, like the rise and fall of ocean waves.

"Happy New Year, Americans! I am your new ruler -- King Robert Ballentine, first of his name," the pirate said with no hint of hoax in his Australian-tinged voice. He could've been saying "I'm your new doctor" -- he made it sound believable.

"President Quigley has been shot in the leg," he continued matter-of-factly. "She is alive and getting the best of care. She will remain alive as long as the old U.S. defense department doesn't try anything heroic and foolish. That means no fighter jets flying around, no aircraft carriers speeding back to the mainland, no troops marching here, there and everywhere. Let's all remain as calm as possible so very few others have to get hurt.

"The Divided States of America is no more," Ballentine declared. "You were so divisive and weak that one man like me -- albeit with considerable help from a powerful backer, some trained killing squads called the 'Black Death,' a bunch of well-placed Benedict Arnolds and some high-tech wizardry -- could catch you with your pants down and kick you up the arse!

"You are now living in the United Kingdom of America, the UKA for short. No more stars and stripes; no more red, white and blue -- quite fittingly, you're flag couldn't even make up its mind what it wanted to be. Well, I've taken care of that for you," Ballentine said, pointing to the black flag over his shoulder. "One color -- black. No more crazy patterns. No more Democrats and Republicans. Democrats, you're all done getting government handouts. You'll have to take care of the poor, old and weak yourselves instead of getting the government to do it for you. Trust me, it'll bring you people closer together when you have to help and rely on one another. You'll truly be united. And you Republicans always wanted less government -- well here I am. I'm getting rid of your executive, legislative and judicial branches effective today and replacing them with me. How's that for downsizing big government? Think of all those bloated salaries we just wiped out. That's my little gift to you. You're welcome."

Bake and Wendy continued to be riveted to the TV screen as Ballentine rambled on in his self-assured manner and baritone voice.

"Hawaii, you're too far away -- consider yourself liberated," the pirate declared. "Do whatever the hell you want, I don't care. Just don't try to come to the rescue. The other 49 former states will now report to 49 royal lords whom I will name within the week. All taxes will be paid to them and, ultimately, to me. I was born and raised in Australia, graduated from the University of Texas in Austin -- that's right, mates, a Longhorn educated right within your nation's borders -- and I've made my fortune as an oil, shipping and media tycoon. That's why I'm such a natural in front of the camera, don't you agree?

"I am a bachelor at the moment, so one of my first tasks will be to find a queen from among your 49 lordships. I will need some heirs, so she must be young, fertile and attractive. She also must be a virgin -- no sloppy seconds for this monarch. We will check for proof of virginity -- that should narrow down the pool of candidates sufficiently. Send an email with your name and a few words on why you want to be my queen, be sure to attach a color photo and/or video, and we'll film a little TV show about me and the five finalists for your viewing pleasure right here on the brand new UKA network. Deadline to enter is April 15 -- also your tax day, right? My web cloud address is kingrobert@queencontest.uka.

"We'll have other fine programming on the UKA network very soon, including an exclusive interview with Margeaux Quigley, your former president, as soon as she's feeling up to it. That should get big ratings. Potential advertisers can email us at kingrobert@sponsorships.uka.

"I think that's enough for now. I know most of you are a bit tipsy from New Year's Eve. Take a pill, drink a glass of water, get some sleep and we'll talk again soon," Ballentine concluded with a broad smile.

The pirate then grabbed a gold crown off the desk behind him, plunked it on top of his head, grinned and signed off with a hearty, "Good night, mates."

"Can you imagine the balls this guy has?" Bake asked as the TV screen returned to a black flag, red background and white letters -- "United Kingdom of America" -- with classical music playing.

"I'd rather not," Wendy said, scrambling back to her desk and scrolling on her tablet computer. "I'm going to Google his name. Robert Ballentine, right?"

"Right," Bake said. "I can't believe this guy -- he's not well."

"That may well be," Wendy said, "but it says here he's practically a trillionaire, and now he just named himself king of the second most powerful country in the world."

"Sounds like someone wants to be his queen," Bake snickered.

"Ah yes … if only I were a virgin," Wendy said with a playful sigh.

Chapter 11

Year(s): Classified
Place: Kingsbury, Nevada

Margeaux Quigley experienced the tidal wave of energy behind her one last time at 11:19 a.m. and she blasted from black into white. When the shaking subsided, she rubbed her eyes to adjust to the brightness and found herself standing, not floating, on a white carpet in a white room with a closed door to her right. The door looked like it was made of tinted glass and it had a gold knob. Margeaux realized her swim cap and vest were gone; so too her smart phone and the zero-gravity effect.

She was also completely naked. Surprisingly, she felt comfortable with that. To her left, she saw a long clothing rack filled with colorful, flowing garments on hangers. She scratched her toes against the fluffy white carpet beneath her feet and walked over to the clothing rack. It was like she was in a dressing room at a fancy mall -- except that as she gathered her bearings, she began to feel slightly nauseous. There was a slight up-and-down motion under her feet, as if she were on board a large ship. But even that felt calming, especially after what she had been through over the last 52 minutes.

Maybe all of this was just a dream. Perhaps Ventana gave us all tranquilizers or something so he wouldn't have to deal with us during detention, she thought.

Either way, Margeaux's anxiety had left her and she felt at peace for the first time in a long time.

Maybe I'm dead. That's possible. I did watch myself get shot.

But Margeaux didn't feel dead. In fact, she smiled as she selected a long, silky blue gown, white slip and blue panties. She put them on and they fit perfectly. Oddly though, there were no shoes.

As she approached the tinted-glass door, Margeaux could see the outline of her reflection as if she were staring into a rolled-up car window. The face looking back at her was young and beautiful -- 17, not the old woman who had become president; her hair was down and longer than she remembered having it, and there was something strange and shiny on top of her head. Could it be a tiara? No, it actually looked more like a crown. She closed her eyes, opened them again and the reflection remained the same. But when she tried to touch the crown, she only felt her hair.

Yes, I must be dead, she thought.

Margeaux fearlessly turned the gold knob on the door with her right hand and opened it. She entered a long, narrow hallway lined with candles on small ledges that jutted out from the walls and a

72

gorgeous carpet that stretched out before her in alternating squares of white and black. At the far end of the hall, she could see the profile of a man standing there. He was dressed all in black with a large face and a dark ponytail. He was not looking at her. He was facing what looked like an open room at the end of the hall and talking to someone else.

Suddenly, Margeaux's heartbeat quickened. The peaceful feeling left her. She clenched her fists and realized she hated this man, but she didn't know why. *Is Ventana the man at the end of the hall? Did that jar head grow out his hair and wear a ponytail now? It can't be him. So who is it then?*

Margeaux took one bare-footed step forward on the checkered rug and noticed the man was wearing a gold crown.

I swear he wasn't wearing a crown one step ago. What the hell is going on?

She also could see the man was not Ventana. She was certain she had never seen him before in her life, and yet she still had the overwhelming urge to confront him.

That's when she sprinted down the hallway in her bare feet with speed she never knew she possessed. She burst upon the pony-tailed man in what seemed like one-tenth of a second. He never saw her coming. She took him by the neck with her right hand and she instinctively knew she could crush his windpipe whenever she wanted. He tried to struggle, but her grip was too strong -- like a grown woman on a little boy. Margeaux wrenched his frightened face toward hers so she could study it

-- she took a mental photograph of every feature, every wrinkle, even the spittle on the left corner of his mouth. His blue eyes were full of terror and she enjoyed that.

Then, with lightning speed, Margeaux released her grip, pushed the man backward a few feet and leveled him in the balls with a savage right-leg kick. The pony-tailed man doubled over in pain and groaned.

One second later, Margeaux grabbed his head, pulled his right ear close to her mouth and heard herself say, "Check, asshole!"

. . .

"Why? What's wrong with your asshole?" the strange-looking man in the white lab coat asked Margeaux as she opened her eyes and realized she was flat on her back -- once again holding her smart phone and wearing her Saturday detention clothes, swim cap and vest. She was trapped inside a glass capsule, a hyperbaric chamber perhaps.

The creepy guy with the long, pointy nose, glasses and balding head was staring at her through the glass like she was some kind of science experiment. Margeaux had no idea who he was or where she was. But when he opened the glass with a switch on the side of the capsule and leaned over her, Margeaux thrust her right hand up in a flash and put his neck in a death grip she never knew she had. She had a strong feeling of déjà vu as the man struggled for air with bulging green eyes. Then two jar heads -- neither of whom was Ventana -- rushed

into the room and came to his rescue. It took both of
them to pull Margeaux's one hand off the creepy
guy's neck. He fell off his mobile stool and writhed
around on the white-tiled floor gasping for air.
Margeaux now began to realize she had nearly
killed the stranger without even thinking twice
about it.

"Two more seconds and he was dead," one jar
head told the other. They looked like twins,
Margeaux observed, as she began climbing out of
the chamber.

"Who are you? Where am I?" Margeaux asked
as the jar head twins warily watched their own
necks, backed away a few feet and allowed her to
slowly stand up next to the chamber. They just
stared at her with nervous brown eyes.

"Answer me!" she demanded.

"Take Dr. Melvin elsewhere so he can recover,
boys," another man in a white lab coat calmly
instructed the jar heads as he opened a white door
and entered the room.

They complied quickly, and suddenly
Margeaux was standing there looking into the face
of another man she had never seen before. He was
tall and handsome with graying brown hair. There
were tears in his blue eyes as he gazed at
Margeaux's beautifully confused, swim-capped
face. They looked at each other for several silent
seconds amid a small laboratory with white walls,
ceilings and floor, numerous computers and
monitors, beige cabinets and the long, glass
chamber from which she had just emerged.

"My name is Bill Cyr," the man said, which drew a squinty look from Margeaux, as if she had heard the name somewhere before.

"Do I know you?" she asked, clawing at her itchy scalp. "And can I finally take this annoying thing off?"

"Yes, of course," Cyr said, helping Margeaux remove her cap and vest. "The answer to your first question is a bit more complicated."

Oh great, here we go again. Another Ventana speaking in riddles, Margeaux thought.

"How about you people just level with me for once and tell me the whole truth," she pleaded.

"I will do exactly that if you feel up to it," Cyr said.

"I'm a little dizzy, but I don't care. I deserve to know why I was kidnapped to God knows where … to God knows when, I should say," Margeaux said.

"Please sit, have a drink of water and a snack," Cyr said, offering her the stool Dr. Melvin had been using and handing her bottled water and a package of peanut butter crackers from his lab coat pocket before pulling up a chair directly across from her. Margeaux tore the wrapper and munched the crackers ravenously, then took a long drink of water. Cyr smiled and looked almost in awe as he watched her. "We'll give you a real meal in about an hour, OK?"

"Why have you been looking at me like that … and the tears earlier? Please tell me the truth. I will get down on my knees and beg if that's what it takes," Margeaux said.

"That won't be necessary," Cyr said. "Let's see, where to begin? You are no longer in 1984."

He paused to see if Margeaux wanted to interrupt, but she waved him on like she knew that already.

"All of it -- I'll try to digest it as you go and I'll ask questions and/or strangle you at the end," Margeaux said quite seriously in between bites of cracker.

"Fair enough," Cyr said, smiling at her blunt threat like he had dealt with the likes of her before. "Margeaux, you arrived here in 52 minutes according to your body clock, but 52 years in reality -- this is March 15, 2036."

Again he paused for a second, but she waved him on.

"How is this possible?" Cyr asked rhetorically. "No technology of ours. We've had some assistance from a highly intelligent life form that I will introduce you to later. We call him a 'he' ... he's more machine than being, but he crashed into the Pacific Ocean in 2033. Our Navy Seals retrieved him and saved him, our scientists got him working again and we've bonded nicely with him over the past two years or so. He is top secret. The hoax in Roswell, New Mexico, back in 1948 has served us well -- sort of like the boy who cried wolf; now when the real thing arrived, no one knew or no one cared to pursue it. The closest translation to his name in English is 'Gatherer.' He comes from a planet orbiting a star within our galaxy, but it's quite a distance away. Last year, for security reasons, we moved him from Area 51 in east

Nevada to here -- Area 52 in west Nevada. We call him 'G52,' or '52' for short."

"Wow," Margeaux said, shaking her head in disbelief and running her hands through her newly liberated hair. Then she remembered the man in black with the ponytail, but she shut the memory off and focused on the conversation at hand. At least this guy appeared to be telling it straight. She wasn't about to lose focus now.

"Wow exactly," Cyr said, looking relieved that Margeaux was handling his bizarre explanation calmly so far. "You arrived here -- beneath your former high school, what is now Area 52 -- via what we call a CAR, or Clone Adaptor Rocket. Not only did we transport you into the future, but we also adapted you along the way. We fed information into your brain about what was happening in the world between 1984 and 2036, updated you about some important people and events in your life, and planted clues about your mission, if you choose to accept it."

"Is this mission impossible?" Margeaux asked with a playful grin.

Cyr laughed, then turned more serious. "It just might be," he said, looking her straight in the eyes.

"Ventana told me I had a mission, too -- where is that asshole anyway?" Margeaux asked bluntly.

Cyr chuckled. "He's here -- recovering from a rough round trip," he said. "He'll need extra time. You'll get to talk to him later."

"I can't wait," Margeaux said sarcastically before she, too, became more serious. "What about

Bake, Danny and the others -- did they really all die?"

Cyr looked somber.

"All are dead except for Jimmy Baker -- he's recovering, too, and you can speak to him later as well," Cyr said.

Margeaux tried to fight off tears as Cyr explained what happened.

"CAR requires a balance of light and dark, positive and negative energy matter to work," he explained, putting a hand on her shoulder. "Five of your classmates were sacrificed to bring you, Ventana, Baker and Capobianco to the future. Ventana roughly weighs twice as much as LaFrance and DiFusco, so five died to bring four forward. We wanted you to have some company here. However, unbeknownst to us, Capobianco died in the 2001 terrorist attacks, so his clone was unable to complete the journey. The balance was compromised along the way and we do expect that you, Baker and Ventana will experience some unexpected side effects as a result."

"Like wanting to strangle people and actually being able to do it," Margeaux said.

"Something like that," Cyr said vaguely. "We'll know more in time."

"But why did my classmates -- jerks though they were -- have to die? What is my mission? What is a clone -- a copy of me? Please continue with this madness," she urged him on with an agitated tone.

Cyr remained calm, empathetic and talked to her softly.

"I don't mean to upset you," he said. "I know this seems like a science fiction movie, but it's very real. … Another thing you should know is that I am your stepson."

"What?" Margeaux responded in shock.

"Technically I'm not your stepson because you are a 17-year-old copy of the woman who married my father," Cyr said. "That woman is President Margeaux Quigley, who will turn 69 on …"

"May 23rd," Margeaux finished his sentence as flashes of the wounded president, first gentleman and the ninja assassins seared her brain. "You're the son of the man who was shot defending the president."

"Yes, Bradley Cyr was my father and the president's husband," Cyr said sadly.

"Was?" Margeaux pressed him softly.

"I'm afraid so," Cyr said.

Margeaux embraced the stranger without even thinking about it and they shared a tearful embrace for several moments. Then she pulled back, not understanding her emotions. Cyr empathized with her reaction and continued.

"There was a coup on New Year's Eve -- many leaders of our government were killed that night and the next day," Cyr said. "Many other members of our government turned out to be traitors, choosing money over loyalty and patriotism. They sold us out to a self-proclaimed king who wears all black and waves a black flag around like he's a pirate. His name is Robert Ballentine. He also goes by the nickname 'Balls.' He's covertly backed by the Chinese, who are the No. 1 superpower in the world these days like we used to be. Also, Ballentine has taken you, President Margeaux Quigley, hostage. You're recovering from a gunshot wound to the right leg."

"My soccer leg," Margeaux interjected bitterly.

"Yes, the same leg you scored a bunch of winning goals with for Stanford University back in the mid- to late-'80s," Cyr told her proudly.

Margeaux allowed herself a small grin as she rubbed her jeans-clad golden right leg with her right hand.

"I will kill Balls if that's what you want me to do," she said boldly, now remembering the black-garbed king's terrified face and how she said the words "check asshole" into his filthy ear. "Is that my mission -- to avenge my own shooting, the coup, my husband, your father?"

"Not exactly," Cyr said, sounding like Ventana for a second. "We were hoping you could help us locate Ballentine and the president. That's the problem. We don't even know where he is. We believe he is on board a ship or he's jumping from ship to ship every night. The Chinese are way ahead of us. They jam our tracking and satellite equipment. And because the president remains Ballentine's hostage, our military options are extremely limited."

"What about the alien? Why can't he figure it out?" Margeaux asked with a hint of annoyance.

"Espionage and war technology is his weakness -- he comes from a planet where beings get along. There's no nationalism, terrorism or war," Cyr explained.

"Maybe he should take us back to his world then," Margeaux said. "But I guess, first, we should find the other me. How do you know Ballentine and the president are on a ship, instead of just down the street?"

"Because he interviewed the president on his TV network about a week after the coup," Cyr said. "The man is a megalomaniac."

"That must've been fascinating to watch," Margeaux said.

"It was, and I'll show you some of it after you've had a real meal and a chance to get acclimated to 2036," Cyr said. "But by analyzing the videotape, we were able to detect a slight ebb and flow, if you will, that seem to indicate he's on the water somewhere. He also hasn't made any public appearances on American soil so far. We think he's playing it safe until his transition of power becomes more complete."

"So where do I come in?" Margeaux asked.

"Well, King Ballentine is seeking a queen," Cyr said with some hesitation in his voice. "And that's where we might be able to exploit his weakness for love with our new, alien technology."

"You want me to be his queen, are you crazy?" Margeaux responded sharply.

"No, we want him to think that you want to be his queen -- it's a trap," Cyr said.

"A trap," Margeaux repeated with a skeptical look, "for him or for me?"

Cyr nodded gravely, as if it could go either way.

"It's a dangerous mission. I'm not going to sugarcoat it," he said. "But if we can embed you into his floating headquarters, we'll be able to track you with a device we plant inside something you'll wear -- like a piece of jewelry. Then we'll know where he is and our special ops team will find a way to take him out. That's what our boys excel at. We're confident that if we kill Ballentine, the whole hostile takeover will collapse. He's the public face of it. He's financing it. He's the head of the snake."

Margeaux's head ached from the 52-year trek, the information overload and the threat to her life. *What ever happened to just being a teenager?*

"But why would this so-called king ever want me for his queen?" she asked. "I'm only 17 for one thing and he's really old."

Cyr smiled at her frank assessment. "He wants an attractive young woman ... a virgin," he said haltingly.

"Disgusting," she said.

"That's why we brought you here before the senior prom in 1984," Cyr said with a slight smirk.

"Why, that's when I lost it?" she asked, blushing. "Who was it? Danny?"

Cyr wasn't going to answer that. He shook his head.

"You can talk to yourself -- President Quigley -- about that, not your stepson," he said with a smile.

"It would be amazing to meet her ... me," Margeaux said.

"She's an amazing woman -- as are you," Cyr said. "You're two different people -- sort of like being identical twins separated by 52 years. Now that you've survived the CAR trip, you will live even if the president dies."

"And if I die … on this mission?" Margeaux asked.

"The president could still live to be 100, who knows?" Cyr said.

"And why would King Ballentine pick me to be his queen out of all the young, attractive virgins in the world?" she asked.

"Because you look like a young President Quigley," Cyr said.

Margeaux seemed confused.

"We will highlight that rare and special quality on your queen contest application," Cyr said, nodding to a jar head just outside the door who was looking in on them through a small glass window in the white door. And just like that Lou Ventana stepped into the room with a small digital camera in his right hand. He wore a white T-shirt, camouflage pants and black boots. Margeaux suddenly shivered with traumatic memories of Saturday detention.

"It's you again," Margeaux said, eyeing his formidable presence bitterly.

Ventana smiled as pleasantly as he could muster.

"Good to see you made it here OK, Miss Quigley," Ventana said. "May I take your photograph?"

"What the hell for?" she protested, shielding her face with her left hand.

Because of Margeaux's obvious and reasonable mistrust of Ventana, Cyr did the talking.

"We'd like to send a high-quality photo from 2036 of *Victoria Kensington*," Cyr said, pausing after the name for emphasis, "alongside a poor-quality photo from 1984 of Margeaux Quigley so the king and his flaks will be wowed by the uncanny resemblance. It will make our contest entry stand out like no other. We've studied this narcissist closely every time he's faced the cameras on his UKA network. He'll be too intrigued not to pick you as one of his five finalists, especially when we play up the striking similarities on your application."

Ventana nodded at her. Margeaux cringed, but then shifted her focus to her new "stepson" instead. There was at least a part of her that felt she could do this for him, for the president, for the murdered first gentleman and for her broken country.

"Victoria Kensington? Is that my …," she asked.

"Alias, yes," Cyr said, putting a hand on her shoulder.

"At least you guys know how to pick out a cool name," Margeaux said with a slight grin. "I'll give you that."

Ventana raised the small camera to take her photograph, but waited for her final approval before pressing the button to turn it on. Margeaux knew in her gut there was no turning back if she agreed to this photograph.

"You better kill him before he tries to have sex with me -- I'm not losing my virginity to an old man with a ponytail and potatoes in his ears -- not in 1984, 2036 or 2084," Margeaux said, pointing at Ventana.

Ventana and Cyr both laughed.

"If you lead us to him, I'll shove a bazooka up his ass and blow his hippy head to 2184," Ventana thundered as only he could.

Ventana and me on the same team? Bizarre. I really must love my country ... my president ... me, Margeaux mused.

Margeaux decided she had a couple of more requests.

"I want to see Jimmy Baker and meet the alien right after this," she said.

"Done," Cyr replied happily. "You can all have lunch together and catch up."

Margeaux's stomach growled at that. She checked her watch. It was 12:08 p.m.

"Also, do you have any lipstick or makeup? I could really use a shower, too. That damn swim cap ruined my hair," she said with convincing blue eyes.

Cyr and Ventana were clearly amused.

"Fair enough," Cyr said. "We'll let you freshen up and then we'll do the photo shoot. Is that an acceptable plan, Miss Kensington?"

"Yes, I accept," Margeaux said.

Chapter 12

Date: March 15, 2036
Place: Aboard the yacht "Sheworthy" in the
Pacific Ocean, 625 miles south-southeast of Hawaii

King Robert Ballentine bared his upper body to
a hot afternoon sun and relaxed poolside on the sky
deck of his 202-foot yacht Sheworthy, which was
knifing westward through choppy seas. He sipped
Captain Morgan rum and coke on the rocks with a
wedge of lime while improving his tan for his future
queen in a white lounge chair beside an oval-shaped
pool. He let his long, wet, dark hair breathe without
a ponytail for a change. Dark sunglasses shaded his
eyes and teal swim trunks covered his large balls,
which were now the stuff of legend.

Balls had proclaimed himself king of America
and seized power without even setting foot on her
soil. The former president was his hostage and the
former U.S. government was in shambles thanks to
the highly coordinated, bloody coup on New Year's
Day, 2036. Chinese-paid North Korean assassin
squads dubbed the "Black Death" murdered
hundreds of congress people, Pentagon staffers,

State and Justice Department workers, state police, national guard soldiers and anyone else who tried to resist or restart the old government. Ballentine's 49 royal lords, also backed by the Black Death, seized control of each state capitol in similar fashion.

Federal and state governments were paralyzed and crippled in a matter of two weeks. Popular protests were put down quickly and violently. Fighter jets, tanks and aircraft carriers were not used against the coup because of Ballentine's repeated on-air threats to kill the president -- whom he had shown and interviewed on his UKA network -- if any major attacks were launched against him and his upstart regime.

Hunted by rabid international journalists and American military spies, Ballentine chose to remain aboard various cruise ships, military vessels, oil barges and yachts until the transition of power was more secure. He hopped from ship to ship via helicopters and harrier jets every couple of nights. A small group of bodyguards, media flaks, camera people and a personal chef traveled with him.

Ballentine preferred to control his subjects from afar during this transition phase with charisma and propaganda via his UKA network -- the only major medium allowed in the country. The Black Death did its level best to take out the rest in violent fashion. Only smaller-market websites and local TV networks were allowed to exist without being targeted by assassin squads; even those were randomly monitored by Ballentine's flaks.

Despite relishing his achievement -- having the balls and means to pull off the greatest coup in world history -- Ballentine longed for the day when he felt safe enough to set foot on his conquered land and wave to his subjects with his American-born queen by his side.

She is the key, he mused. *If I pick the right queen, they will love her, and then they just might learn to love me. In time, they will get used to the idea of a monarchy. Their democracy was broken anyway. They always loved the British royals -- what could be better than having your own royal family to love and follow?*

Ballentine's top media flak, Howard Nelson, approached him poolside with a whimsical look on his face. He was in his 30s, thin, with short brown hair, glasses and an Ivy League smugness about him. Ballentine's field marshal of mind control and subject relations, Nelson wore a tropical shirt with khaki shorts and light brown sandals; several high-tech gadgets were holstered around his sand-colored belt.

"We've got a beauty dangling on the line, King Robert," Nelson told Balls as he made a gesture with both hands to indicate the size of the fish. He held a smart phone in his left hand as he did this.

"Oh yeah, mate, let me see," Balls said, taking off his sunglasses and reaching for Nelson's phone.

Nelson hunched down and looked over Ballentine's shoulder as he scrolled the touch screen to the latest contest entry emails.

"This one," Nelson said, pointing at the screen. "Victoria Kensington. Look at the two photos. She looks like former President Quigley's long lost sister -- only she's 17. It's amazing!"

Balls studied the two images attached to the entry email. Both were color photos, but the one on the left was grainy and old. It was a Kingsbury High School yearbook photo of President Margeaux Quigley shot in 1983, during the summer before her senior year. She had an awkward smile, braces on her teeth, shy blue eyes and her black hair partially pinned up with white barrettes. The photo on the right was practically life-like, clearly taken with a high-resolution digital camera from 2036 or thereabouts. Victoria Kensington's face was nearly a mirror image of President Quigley at 17, but Victoria had a confident, almost saucy smile with no braces, enticing blue eyes and straight black hair down past her athletic-looking shoulders. Her hot pink shirt revealed just enough cleavage to stir Balls' swim trunks.

"That's a contender," Ballentine said with a chuckle as he wiped some sweat off his glistening brow. "I might have to take a dip in the pool to cool off."

"Wait, it gets better," Nelson tittered as he moved the screen down and showed Balls the email's text. "Read what Victoria wrote."

Ballentine grinned at his flak and eagerly read the small print.

"I want to be your queen so bad I'll lose my virginity to you on your TV show," the text said. "And because I just happen to look like a young President Quigley, it'll be like you're fucking America for real -- literally and figuratively!! LOL!!!"

Balls howled in lusty delight and slapped Nelson on the back so hard he almost lurched head-first into the pool. "She's a finalist and probably the winner just for that, mate!" he shouted. "You better make damn sure she's on the 'Rendezvous Two' on Tuesday. How many have I picked so far?"

"Three others, king," Nelson said.

"Howie, you pick the fifth finalist from the remaining pool of candidates. I don't care if she's a toothless hag," Balls bellowed as he stood up and prepared to belly flop into the pool. "Let's get this show on the road, mate! It's high time we crowned a queen and showed up in our new United Kingdom of America."

"I will do so, king," Nelson said.

"Good, now go, so I can jump into the pool and handle my balls," Ballentine said with a raspy laugh before plunging into the deep end and sending a tsunami of ripples onto the sky deck.

Chapter 13

Date: March 15, 2036
Place: Area 52, Kingsbury, Nevada
After her shower in a white, pristine bathroom somewhere in the secretive underground labyrinth of Area 52, Margeaux Quigley dolled up her hair and brushed on some makeup; donned a hot pink shirt, tight blue jeans and sexy black boots, and gave Cyr and Ventana the photo shoot they wanted. She enjoyed acting like a different young woman named Victoria Kensington -- it was a nice escape from her completely fucked-up, clone-crazed existence.

Margeaux was not happy, however, when Ventana refused to let her see what he wrote in the queen contest application email. Heck, she was still coming to grips with the concept of electronic mail, never mind what words the jar head used on her behalf. His familiar, creepy grin hinted that he conjured up plenty of unseemly words to entice the so-called king. But, indeed, that was the mission she chose to accept. Now she must help lure the megalomaniac into the trap -- the sooner, the better, so she could get on with her own new life 52 years in the future. She was eager to emerge from the Area 52 bunker, breathe fresh air and gaze at the sky again.

But right now, with the Black Death always a threat, she was safer in Area 52, Cyr said. The death squads had forcibly taken over Area 51 in the early days of the coup, but so far had left the lesser known Area 52 alone. In fact, the Black Death had backed off on killings in general over the last several weeks. They had switched from offensive mode to defensive mode, targeting only troublemakers and leaving everyone else alone.

Margeaux wanted to see her mother, still very much alive, 89 years old and residing in Arizona now. She also longed to see her 67-year-old brother, who now lived in Oregon. But first, Cyr told her, she must play the role of Victoria Kensington and help make her family's country whole again.

An elite soccer player and competitor with a deep reserve of courage from which to draw strength, Margeaux channeled all of that into her new persona of Victoria Kensington. She also knew that her leap into the future had changed her physically and mentally. She felt powerful -- like every cell in her body had been juiced up to a super level of strength and efficiency. And her mind raced ahead of real time, keenly sensing what would happen and what others around her were thinking, feeling and planning to do before they thought, felt and did them. That's why she got upset with Ventana. She never actually saw the text of the email he sent to Ballentine, but she felt he had wronged her. She knew he had used words that would make her feel like a slut. She was a virgin, not a whore. She desperately desired to kick Ventana's ass, but the mission had to be the focus now.

A lunch of burgers, fries and Cokes with classmate Jimmy Baker -- something that never would've happened in 1984 -- proved fun and refreshing in 2036. They quickly bonded over their mutual leap into the future and bizarre existence as clones of themselves. Bake, as he liked to be called, wore a new white-and-blue-striped golf shirt, khaki shorts, brown sandals and no swim cap over his short, reddish-brown hair. He, too, glowed brighter after a shower and seemed to have a 52-year bounce in his step.

"My original guy is a journalist up in Reno, Bill told me," Bake said. "I'll probably get to meet up with him after this whole coup blows over. That would be far out."

As usual, Bake accentuated the positive. His dancing blue eyes, red freckles and unmitigated enthusiasm rubbed off on Margeaux. She would try to keep a positive attitude like Bake. What else could she really do anyway? She would play these strange cards she was dealt with the best of her new super abilities, and hopefully everything would come up aces in the end.

That's when the alien rolled into the small, white-walled lunch room. G52 took a spot at the head of their rectangular beige table, where Margeaux and Bake sat across from one another. Part ape-like creature, part robot, G52 had a football-like head with short black fur in the front and metal in the back; four digital-green eyes, two in the front and two in the back; two small holes below the front eyes; a sub-human-sized body with black fur; an overhauled, metallic midsection that looked more machine than alien mammal; two furry, four-fingered hands on two proportional furry arms; and two hairy, four-toed feet on seemingly nonfunctioning furry legs. G52 was encased and transported by a four-wheel, rover-like machine contoured to his seated body. His voice was a machine-altered monotone, emanating from a small speaker on his metallic neck. There was a custom-built device inside him translating his speech into English.

Margeaux and Bake gazed in wonder at the creature as Cyr popped his head into the room for an introduction.

"Margeaux and Jimmy, meet Gatherer 52, aka G52, aka 52, from a planet we call Doron-c and which 52 calls Vel-Zel. Our closest translation of that would be 'origin.'"

"Hello, 52," Bake and Margeaux said in harmony.

"Hello," the alien responded with a slight delay between syllables. Its digital green eyes did not blink, but the creature did raise its left hand in a greeting gesture.

"I'll let you all chat and get acquainted," Cyr said, popping back into the corridor.

"Want a fry, 52?" Bake asked, smiling and pointing to a French fry on his plate in an attempt to break the intergalactic ice.

"I cannot function on this," 52 replied haltingly.

"What do you eat?" Margeaux asked.

"Plant matter, oils and sulfur," 52 stated.

"Sounds delicious," Bake cracked with a playful grin.

"What's Vel-Zel like?" Margeaux asked the alien.

"Bigger than Earth," 52 said. "It has two of what you call sun and three of what you call moon -- what you call sky almost always bright."

"Why did you come to Earth?" Bake asked.

"I was one of thousands of gatherers sent out to collect knowledge -- all one-way missions," 52 said.

I can relate, Margeaux mused. *I'm probably on a one-way mission, too.*

"Humans are helping this gatherer send signals back to Vel-Zel with indication of my location coordinates," 52 continued. "Some of my parts damaged in crash. Some of my parts replaced with human machine parts."

"How did you bring us to this point in time?" Margeaux asked, gesturing to herself and Bake.

"Difficult to answer," 52 said.

"Try us," Bake prodded.

"Do you understand computer machines with intelligence far exceeding human brain parts?" 52 asked.

"We barely had computers in 1984," Margeaux said.

"You, young Margeaux human, are like earlier version of same computer file that is now older and more complete. We retrieve earlier version of file --

that is you -- and bring you forward to copy or replace older version."

Bake scratched his forehead. "How the hell did you do that?"

"Black threads, white threads, space-time tunnels, alternate-plane phenomena are experienced," the alien replied.

"The virtual chessboard?" Margeaux asked.

"The humans here enjoy chess. Now I enjoy chess," 52 said.

"Wait, did you code up our trip that way? Why not Scrabble or Monopoly? And why not kill off a few more people along the way?" Margeaux asked bitterly.

"Chess alternate plane phenomena closely matched with mission of retrieval target … that would be you, Margeaux human, earlier version," 52 stated.

"Well, personally, I would've preferred poker over chess and nobody dying," Margeaux said testily.

"Some day soon you may hold all 52 cards in deck," the alien said.

"Huh?" Margeaux said, shaking her head. Bake just looked dazed.

"Will somebody please tell me what the heck ET is talking about and when we can phone home 1984-style?" Bake finally asked with a gasp and a shoulder shrug.

Margeaux allowed herself a slight grin at Bake's ability to keep a sense of humor. The poor kid was dragged along purely as excess baggage on the CAR trip all because of her and he had no clue why, unlike her. But at least he survived the trip.

"Again, why did my classmates -- the five white pawns -- have to die?" she pressed the alien.

"Matter converted to dark energy. Negative energy density required for some of CAR propulsion," 52 stated matter-of-factly.

"Car? What car?" Bake asked with wide eyes and extra-red freckles. "And why tease me with a swim cap and no water?"

"Clone Adaptor Rocket -- the CAR trip -- Cyr called it," Margeaux explained to her slightly more bewildered classmate.

"Oh, that really clears it up for me, thanks," Bake said sarcastically. Apparently even Bake's positivity had its limits.

"Enough already. This sci-fi shit is beyond us and America is falling apart above us," Margeaux said with an exasperated tone.

"Yeah, Cyr told me – this is not well … not well at all," Bake said. "If only we had not busted Mrs. Pina's balls, we wouldn't have been sent to Saturday detention, Captain Lou wouldn't have hijacked our CAR to 2036 and America would still be the home of the free, right?"

52 kicked his rover into reverse and wheeled toward the door.

"Nice to meet you, earlier-version humans," the alien said in parting.

"Same here, 52 -- that's quite a compliment," Bake replied with another dose of sarcasm.

Margeaux put her suddenly throbbing head in her hands.

"What's the matter Margeaux?" Bake asked.

"So we busted Mrs. Pina's balls. Why does everything have to come back to balls? I'm so sick of balls … and now I have a splitting headache," she said, clawing at her long, fine black hair.

Bake patted her on the shoulder.

"Hey, some day we'll look back on all of this and laugh, right?" he reassured her. "I mean it's not every day I get to have lunch with a very pretty girl and meet an alien."

Margeaux forced herself to pick up her aching head and smile at that.

"Yeah, it's also not every day when 52 years seem to fly by in 52 minutes and that's actually the case," she said, swiping a fry off Bake's plate -- the very same fry he had offered to the alien. "At least they still have French fries in 2036. Thank God for small miracles in these dark times."

Chapter 14

Date: March 15, 2036
Place: Area 52, Kingsbury, Nevada
Cyr and Ventana escorted Margeaux to a new room that evening as they gradually expanded her access to more areas in the largely sealed-off subterranean Area 52 complex.

The U.S. government seized control of the Kingsbury High School property shortly after the bizarre deaths of five students there in 1984 and let the place mostly lie fallow until 2005. By 2017, the entire complex had been completely transformed and the basement level expanded into a much smaller, top-secret offshoot of Area 51 in east Nevada. The upper two levels, more for show than anything else, were occasionally used by lower-rung naval and Defense Department officials for meetings and training seminars. Meanwhile, a new Kingsbury High School had opened across town for the 1985-86 school year and was still going strong as it celebrated its 50th anniversary in 2036. Despite his ongoing attempt at regime change in America,

King Ballentine did allow schools and normal business to resume in the country within three weeks of his coup.

Cyr and Ventana ushered Margeaux, aka Victoria Kensington, into a long L-shaped room with navy blue walls, dark brown carpeting and a chestnut conference table that nearly filled the long part of the L. There were no windows in any of the rooms Margeaux had seen so far, but this one at least had a beautiful full-color digital screen view of Lake Tahoe overlooking the war-room-style table. The short part of the L was Area 52's attempt at a movie room, with a semicircle of bulky, black leather chairs facing a wall of TV monitors.

The two men flanked Margeaux as they all sat down and were greeted by a massive bowl of buttered popcorn and three Cokes on the rectangular coffee table in front of the chairs. Wearing a light blue collared shirt, khaki pants and no lab coat, Cyr pushed a button on a black remote control and all the TV monitors retreated behind a wood exterior except for the huge flat screen in the center.

"Neat trick," Margeaux said, smiling and tying her hair back into a ponytail. She wanted to match King Balls hairstyle for hairstyle as they scouted him before her mission. Balls had chosen Victoria Kensington to be one of his five finalists for queen within an hour of Ventana sending the email application and photos. Cyr had predicted Balls would take the bait and he was correct, but the speed of the positive response definitely took him by surprise. Perhaps the king wasn't getting many applicants.

Whatever the case, Cyr now had to scramble to transform Miss Quigley into Miss Kensington before driving her to the airport in Las Vegas in 48 hours. From there, Ballentine's recruiting agent would meet with all five finalists before putting them on one of 10 private jets that would take off within minutes of each other for an unknown destination. That's when the shell game would begin in earnest. Cyr told Victoria to expect to be re-routed numerous times via all different modes of transportation during the journey to Ballentine's floating headquarters.

Not a big fan of flying, Margeaux surprisingly dreaded the start of the mission more than the destination at this point. In fact, as she was about to view Ballentine on TV for the first time -- announcing his five finalists for queen in prime time on his UKA network -- there was a part of her that was excited to tangle with this formidable foe and defeat him. Her competitive nature was one of her best assets in this dangerous game she was about to play.

Cyr told Margeaux that, after viewing Ballentine's queen finalist announcement, he wanted to show her some excerpts of the king's interview with President Quigley, which had aired on January 8, 2036. Margeaux was so anxious to see that video that she hoped Balls would make the queen finalist segment mercifully brief.

As a commercial for Foster's beer aired on the massive flat screen TV in front of her, Margeaux snuck a peripheral glance at Ventana as he munched on his popcorn in a white T-shirt, fatigues and black boots. He had been especially quiet and cold to her even though she had fully accepted the mission and even gussied up for his photo shoot. She still yearned to confront him, sensing in her gut that she could kick his ass despite his significant size advantage and Navy Seals training. Margeaux's heart quickened at the thought.

I've got to get this guy alone at some point. Captain Lou deserves some corporal punishment. He'd be the perfect punching bag to warm up on before the mission. Wait! Why do I think I can kick his ass? This is crazy. He's a Navy Seal. He'll kill me.

Margeaux's rollercoaster thoughts were suddenly interrupted by the larger-than-life face she had photographed in her memory once before. It was Robert Ballentine staring directly at her -- the long, salt-and-pepper hair pulled into a ponytail behind his bulldog head; the icy blue eyes; the pug nose; the full lips; the mustache and goatee.

Balls beamed at the camera wearing a sharp black power suit with a solid fire-engine-red tie. Is he trying to be the devil incarnate? He leaned against a huge oak desk with his arms folded across his chest and owned the lens with his presence. As an introductory classical music score blared from the surround-sound speakers above her, Margeaux watched Ballentine's every move. He reached for his gold, bejeweled crown on the desk and placed it on his head -- almost like Mr. Rogers donning his sweater before that popular 20th century children's show. Unlike the well-intended Mr. Rogers, however, Balls was trying to hypnotize his subjects with props and pageantry, pirate magnetism and propaganda.

"Good evening United Kingdom of America and a happy Ides of March to you all, mates," Balls said with his Australian charm on full blast. "Tonight I have a brief word to share. I have chosen my five finalists for queen of the kingdom. You'll be able to see them jockey for the crown beginning on Wednesday at 10 p.m. New York time right here on the UKA network.

"There should be plenty of drama as we film the whole process of me selecting your new queen and mine. I will let you, the audience, text in your votes along the way. I will take those votes into consideration as I make my choice because you and I both will have to live with her -- unless, of course, she turns out to be truly awful," he said with a scrunched-up face and a laugh. "In that case, we could always try again. But hopefully, we'll get a fantastic queen in our first go at it. For a preview, I leave you with names and photos flashing across your screen of the five lucky young women who claim to be virgins and who thirst for the title of queen. We shall see who ultimately prevails in Thursday night's live finale show. That's also at 10 o'clock New York time right here on the UKA network. Good night."

As Ballentine signed off, the classical music returned to flood the viewing room and Margeaux stared at the faces of the four young women, one after another, whom she would be meeting soon: Sandy Peck, 18, of St. Louis, a buxom girl with strawberry blond hair, blue eyes and a playful smile; Georgia Fulmer, 19, of Fayetteville, N.C., a black-haired beauty with green eyes and perfect white teeth; Lucy Sanchez, 17, of Los Angeles, with curly brown hair and sexy chocolate eyes, and Jessica Meyers, 18, of Fort Lauderdale, Fla., with wavy reddish-brown hair, hazel eyes, a perfect tan and a long nose that detracted from her otherwise perfect features.

And then Margeaux saw the face that Balls had saved for last -- Victoria Kensington, 17, of Newport, R.I.

"Where am I from?" Margeaux asked Cyr.

"Well, you couldn't be from Kingsbury, Nevada, just like the president, so we picked a place in New England by the ocean," Cyr said. "You come from old money and your ancestors lived in the mansions by the water -- a place worthy of Victoria Kensington. You'll be flying out to visit your old Uncle Bill near Lake Tahoe before heading up to the Las Vegas airport on Monday night. At least that's what Lou wrote in your email."

Margeaux rolled her eyes. *Yeah, that's the very least of what he wrote, I'm sure.*

"You better tell me a lot more about Victoria before this so-called king plays 20 questions with me," she said as Ventana reached for more popcorn and seemingly ignored their conversation.

"We'll do that all day tomorrow," Cyr said.

"Good," she said. "Now show me Balls' interview with the president."

"At once," Cyr said, hitting some buttons on his remote control. "Here's an interesting segment."

Ballentine's face appeared again on the large flat screen TV. It was a close-up shot as he was sitting in a chair. He had to be facing the president because it looked like he was probing her face as he posed the question.

"When did it hit you that your country had become so vulnerable to a hostile takeover -- before, during or after the coup?" Balls asked with a healthy dose of swagger in his baritone voice.

The camera switched to gray-haired President Quigley with her dour and defiant blue eyes. She was sitting in a wheelchair but otherwise looked relatively healthy considering all she had been through. And now she had to endure being interviewed as a hostage for the whole world to see by the very man who had orchestrated her overthrow.

Young Margeaux seethed as she leaned forward in her chair and hung on every word her other self said.

"Our country has been in decline for a long time -- sticking our nose in places we didn't belong, wasting money fighting useless wars, policing the world and neglecting our core. We lost touch with our heart, soul and brains somewhere along the way," the president said, pointing to her head.

"It's just too bad we didn't wake up and do something about it before someone evil like you came along and orchestrated the murders of so many good people," she added in disgust.

Ballentine's blue eyes danced with amusement as the camera switched back to him. He was delighted at the prospect of a spirited verbal joust with his prey.

"But how good could those people truly have been if they were the leaders of a country going in totally the wrong direction?" he asked with a smirk.

The deposed president bristled. So did young Margeaux as she watched.

"So they deserved to be rounded up and shot in cold blood during holiday parties by a bunch of cowards dressed in black?" Quigley asked with venomous eyes and tone. "I deserved to be shot in the leg? My husband deserved to be killed because you're going to fix America -- is that where you're going with this insane interview, you madman?"

Young Margeaux was impressed with her older self -- the way she fought off tears while talking about First Gentleman Bradley Cyr and battled with her captor on every word.

"I'm not sure *deserve* is the right term," Balls countered, "but surely something needed to change at the top. Sometimes a good purge can go a long way."

President Quigley glared at Ballentine for a moment as the camera fixed on her.

"Who cares what you think?" she finally said, angrily. "You're a pirate and a murderer. You're a coward who doesn't even have the *balls* to set foot on your so-called conquered territory. You let China do all the dirty work. You paid them billions so they'd let you play with your foolish crown. You're nothing but a puppet, understood? You're a puppet, not a pirate."

Again Balls beamed. Perhaps he was tallying the record TV ratings and advertising dollars inside his thick skull.

"Oh, I'll be taking up residence in the kingdom soon enough," he said with a cocky smile. "Then we'll see who is a puppet. I will be king and you will be the lamest president in the history of your country -- the one who let the nation and the Constitution be ripped away during her watch. I will right America's sinking ship far better than you or any of your useless former legislators ever could. King Robert Ballentine, the first of his name, will go down in history as the savior of that long-neglected land."

Cyr turned off the interview at that moment, letting Margeaux chew on Balls' words. The strategy worked. Margeaux lurched forward and violently flung the bowl of popcorn across the room. Even the normally cool Ventana was taken aback by the 17-year-old girl's reaction. Cyr was not surprised. His stepmother, President Margeaux, also had a bit of a temper when provoked.

"I will take him down!" Margeaux shouted, pointing at the dark TV screen.

"Relax," Ventana finally spoke. "We just need you to lead us to him. We'll take care of the rest."

Margeaux angrily glared at Ventana like he was an enemy, too. Cyr spoke evenly and tried to calm her down.

"Yes, we'll provide you with jewelry that can be tracked with GPS technology and ...," Cyr said, stopping abruptly when he noticed Margeaux slump back into her chair. Her eyes rolled back and she began to shake -- a little at first, but quickly turning into convulsions.

"She's having a seizure!" Cyr yelled as he and Ventana jumped up to tend to her. "Quick, get her to the chamber and I'll send Dr. Melvin at once, assuming he's still up for it after what she did to him last time. It must be ill effects from the leap forward."

Ventana scooped up Margeaux in his burly arms, carried her out of the L-shaped room and down the gleaming white corridor. The queen finalist already needed medical attention, yet her dangerous mission hadn't even begun.

Chapter 15

Date: March 16, 2036
Place: Area 52, Kingsbury, Nevada

Margeaux woke up at nearly 6 a.m. on Sunday with an annoying sense of déjà vu. She was back in the hyperbaric chamber, staring through the glass at the creepy Dr. Melvin again. He was leering right back at her with his probing pupils. The only difference this time was he didn't ask what was wrong with her asshole.

Margeaux's seizures had stopped, but a dull ache still bothered her head and her mood was foul.

"Get me out of here!" she snapped at Dr. Melvin. "I promise I won't try to kill you this time."

"I would appreciate that, but do you really feel up to it?" the bald man with the white lab coat and beady brown eyes asked as his glasses hung from the tip of his long, pointy nose.

"I do, but better yet, can you send for Lou Ventana? I need a few words with him alone about my mission," Margeaux requested.

"As you wish," Dr. Melvin said, paging Ventana with one button after fishing a smart phone out of his lab coat pocket.

Ventana arrived two minutes later looking half asleep and inconvenienced by the interruption. Margeaux pulled herself out of the chamber, slowly stood up and rubbed the sleep out of her own eyes.

"Miss Quigley said she would like a word with you alone about her mission," Dr. Melvin informed the jar head.

"Fine," Ventana said tersely as Dr. Melvin got up from his little five-wheel stool and departed.

"Close the door," Margeaux ordered Ventana as she recalled flashbacks of him locking the door behind her in Room C. He eyed her a bit warily but complied.

"What's the problem and why the urgency at 6 o'clock on a Sunday?" he asked, folding his arms in front of his chest. He stood four feet away from her in the 20-by-12-foot rectangular, windowless lab full of computers, medical monitors and equipment, two hospital gurneys and one hyperbaric chamber. Ventana was still wearing his white T-shirt, fatigues and black boots. Margeaux still wore her hot pink short-sleeve shirt and blue jeans with white socks and no shoes.

"What did you write about me in that electronic mail to Ballentine that made him pick me so fast? I want to know right now," Margeaux said with blazing blue eyes as she adjusted her ponytail and acted like she was ready for a physical confrontation if necessary. Ventana allowed himself a grin at the prospect of tangling with the thin, athletic girl.

"The objective was to get him to pick you and that objective was achieved -- that's all the matters," the Navy Seal said flatly, looking her squarely in the eyes.

"Tell me what you wrote so I won't be surprised when Balls gets me alone or asks me about it on live TV for all I know," Margeaux persisted, trying a different tack.

Ventana smiled and gave in.

"I texted him that you look like a younger version of the president so when you'd fuck, it would look like he was fucking America -- literally and figuratively," he said, injecting a little edge into his voice on the expletives.

"I also wrote that you were dying to fuck him on live TV," Ventana added with a much nastier tone and an obscene hip thrust to drive home the point.

Margeaux decked Ventana so fast he didn't even have time to finish his second hip thrust. She kicked him in the balls with her right foot so hard he doubled over. She reached down with her right hand, grabbed his barrel-shaped neck and threw him into a white wall. Ventana bounced off the wall, crashed into a computer monitor, hit his head on the edge of a wooden desk and fell to the white, tiled floor in a heap. He immediately tried to protect his face, but Margeaux swept down on him too fast. She pummeled the jar head with a super-rapid right-left-right combination of punches to the nose and forehead. She hit him with a force he never could've expected from a 5-foot-8, 120-pound girl. His nose was bloodied and his head was woozy from the blows. He just lay on the floor with his hands up in a defensive position and looked dazed.

"Stop!" he managed to say as Margeaux loomed over him ready to resume the barrage whenever she wanted. Instead, she elected to abuse him verbally.

"Captain Lou Ventana," she said with a sneer. "Your last name means window in Spanish and you work in a place with no goddamn windows -- that's fucking rich, isn't it?

"You kidnap little kids, drag some of them into the future, kill some of them off to feed your alien chess maniac and all the while seem to enjoy it a little too much, don't you!" she yelled down into his shell-shocked face. "Now I've got headaches, seizures and God knows what's next from jumping 52 years in 52 minutes -- all so I can do your dirty work and kill Balls."

Ventana held his left hand up toward her and tried to speak.

"Just shut up and stay on the floor!" she thundered as blood coursed through her veins. "I'll do it. I know in my gut I won't get any backup from you and your team. It's all on me -- the expendable clone -- to get this guy."

"But ...," Ventana said.

"It's my turn to talk," she cut him off. "I'm in charge now, not you. I'm in control. You had your fun kidnapping people, killing people and making me sound like a whore -- which I am not," she said, pounding her chest with tears in her eyes.

113

"I've seen flashes of what's going to happen. I know it's all on me. That's fine. I'll handle it. But I just want you to know that I'm not fine with you, Ventana, and your *leadership*. Got that?" she said, pointing down at him.

Ventana gazed up at her and nodded silently like a little boy in timeout for bad behavior. He was in awe of her physical power and complete dominance in this moment. The multiple CAR trips had badly weakened him, while Margeaux was superhuman after her one leap forward, he deduced. His head stung, his nose likely was broken and no words came easily, but he managed a few, in a much humbler tone, as he lay under her fiery glare.

"I have them, too," Ventana mumbled.

Margeaux saw he was acting like a schoolyard bully who had been whipped. She softened her tone, unclenched her fists and let her blood simmer down from a boil.

"Have what?" she asked.

Ventana put his left hand on his bruised head.

"Headaches and seizures," he said. "From the round trip."

Margeaux suddenly and unexpectedly felt a pang of empathy for the Navy Seal at her feet.

"Then I better make this all worth it," she said with smoldering resolve.

Chapter 16

Date: March 17, 2036
Place: Area 52, Kingsbury, Nevada

The teenager dazzled in an emerald cocktail dress that showed off her toned arms and legs and offered a hint of cleavage. Her black hair was pinned up in an elegant twist and her 5-foot-8 frame was pumped up to 6 feet with 4-inch emerald heels. She glittered with diamond earrings, a necklace and a bracelet on her left wrist. She also wore an emerald ring on her left hand.

"You are a vision -- a St. Patrick's Day charmer, Miss Kensington," Cyr said with a proud smile as Margeaux Quigley, aka Victoria Kensington, finally emerged from the Area 52 bunker, her former high school, and stepped out into the fresh air of a dry, warm Nevada evening. A black stretch limousine waited for her at the bottom of a horseshoe-shaped drive that took authorized vehicles in and out of the gated complex.

This could be my prom night, but it's a long, long way from that, Victoria thought, as she walked toward a very uncertain fate.

A friendly faced driver in a tuxedo held the rear door open for Victoria as she ducked into the limo and made herself comfortable on a plush burgundy-colored seat. The driver let Cyr join her before closing the door and taking the wheel. He shut the automatic window separating him from Cyr and Victoria so they could chat in private during the several-hour trip to the airport in Las Vegas.

"Some wine to calm the nerves?" Cyr offered as he readied two glasses while sitting across from Victoria and next to the limo's mini wet bar. He wore a white-collared long-sleeve shirt, gold wrist watch, gray slacks and black shoes.

"Yes, definitely," Victoria said as the limo began to move.

They each sipped a fine-tasting California red and didn't know what to say for several minutes. Cyr's face looked worn out from stress and grief, though he smiled through it often. He was a good actor, just like Victoria would have to be on this mission.

"Was … is Margeaux a good stepmother to you -- a good wife to your father?" Victoria asked, finally breaking the silence and only feeling bold enough to pose such a question because she was now forced to be a new person with a new identity.

Cyr seemed visibly caught off guard by her question, but he pondered it for a moment and tears filled his soft blue eyes. He smiled anyway.

"I'm sorry," Victoria said, leaning forward and putting her hand on his.

"Don't be," Cyr said, taking a sip of wine and a deep breath. "She was … is … the best stepmother

116

and wife that a son and husband could hope for. That's why this is killing me -- to feel so helpless to find her, rescue her from this egotistical maniac and save the country."

"I will see her very soon and I will find a way to tell her you are doing your best to do exactly that," Victoria assured him. "I mean, you've certainly gone above and beyond to bring me here -- to even come up with such a scheme is genius. It's just too bad my classmates had to die to make it happen."

"Yes, a very unfortunate means to an end indeed," Cyr said somberly. "If there were other ways to get this guy, believe me, we would've tried them. But Ballentine holds the president's life in his hands. He's calling the shots. We can't just storm every ship in the ocean and take him out when he's made it clear he will kill her. We're basically playing the only card he's dealt us -- the queen card. That's the opening we've got right now and we've got to take it. You're already a national hero in my book for accepting this risky mission. I will pray every second that you remain safe. Age 17 or not, I don't want to lose my stepmother twice in three months."

"I'll find a way to get this guy. I promise you that," Victoria said, her sudden wine buzz making her feel even bolder.

"Just throw down the popcorn and we'll follow the GPS trail," Cyr said with a grin, recalling her reaction to Balls on video.

Victoria smiled for a second, too, but then she bit her lip.

"Like you said though, even if I lead you to him, he will kill the president if Ventana and his team try to attack him," Victoria said.

"Knowing where you and the president are is the crucial first step," Cyr said. "At least then we would have a chance to set something up. The Seals are the best at these types of operations. We could find a way to get one sharpshooter onboard at some point and take him out. And if we kill the head, the whole snake just might die. I know in my heart my stepmother wants us to get Ballentine one way or the other. She very well may die in the operation, but we'll make damn sure he does, too. He needs to pay for what he's done to my father and so many others. There's no way we can allow him to turn our democracy into his own personal monarchy. The time to act begins now."

"I've seen flashes that I might be able to take Ballentine out myself," Victoria said. "I'm feeling stronger since the CAR trip. … I'm talking *a lot* stronger."

"Yes, I saw the results on Lou's face," Cyr said with a slight grin.

Victoria looked down at her bruised right knuckle, feeling embarrassed.

"And G52 said something about me holding all the cards in the deck. What did he mean by that?" she asked, looking up at Cyr again.

"I'm not going to lie to you, Miss Kensington," Cyr said. "You're a very special young lady with some very special abilities that even we aren't sure how they will manifest themselves in the coming days. But you are not a trained killer. This

Ballentine will be surrounded by trained killers. Be extremely patient and do not overestimate what you can do. If you see a golden opportunity, I'm not going to sit here and try to talk you out of it. But you better be 150 percent sure about it -- because we may never get another chance. Understood?"

"In chess, the queen is far more deadly than the king," Victoria said. "I'll show Balls which game I'm playing."

"This is no game," Cyr said sternly.

"For me, from this point on, it has to be," Victoria said, "because that's when I'm at my best."

Chapter 17

Date: March 17, 2036
Place: Las Vegas, Nevada

Dozens of members of the Black Death manned armed checkpoints all around the perimeter of McCarran International Airport in Las Vegas on this particular evening. The only flights allowed into the airfield that day carried the other four contestants vying to be King Ballentine's queen. The only flights allowed out were 10 private jets scheduled to take off in two-minute intervals between 11:30 p.m. and 11:50 p.m.

Victoria Kensington's black limousine arrived at the main checkpoint at 10:17 p.m. Eight black-hooded ninjas, armed with large automatic rifles, surrounded the limo from a short distance away while two far less scary people actually stepped forward to greet the vehicle's occupants. One young man went to the rear of the limo to join the driver in unloading Victoria's two suitcases and a personal bag. The other older man opened the limo door, and helped her and Cyr step out onto the sidewalk that was within walking distance of the main terminal.

"Welcome, my name is Bruce Walker and I'll be assisting you with the queen contest transportation process from this point forward," the short, 40-something man said with an Australian accent as he shook their hands. Victoria noticed him nervously checking her out, up and down. He had tightly cropped curly brown hair, a bald spot on top of his head and bad teeth. His charcoal-colored suit didn't quite match his jet-black shoes and he smelled of cheap musk.

"Well I guess this is it," Cyr said, embracing Victoria warmly and eyeing Walker warily before retreating a few steps. "Best of luck, my niece. The next time I see you perhaps you will be queen."

Victoria smiled, trying to pretend it was all just some crazy beauty pageant.

"Thanks, I'll do my best, Uncle Bill," she said, gazing almost tearfully at him as he waved to her and ducked back into the limo. She hoped this wasn't the last time she'd see him. She blew Cyr a kiss before his face -- perhaps the last friendly visage she would see for a long time -- vanished behind the window's rising tinted glass.

"Come this way, Miss Kensington, is it?" Walker said with a less than masculine voice.

Victoria hesitated for a second, then began walking alongside the man who was several inches shorter than her.

"Yes, I'm Victoria Kensington," she said, more to confirm it in her own mind. *No slip-ups from here on,* she warned herself.

The younger man carting her bags led the way as she and Bruce Walker followed him through the automatic door together and entered the airport's deserted main terminal.

"You are the last of the five contestants to arrive, so Dr. Foley will see you right away," Walker said, motioning her to the right as the man carting her bags veered to the left.

"Why do I have to see a doctor? And where is he taking my bags?" Victoria asked as her heartbeat quickened and her head began to ache.

"All of your questions will be answered very shortly, Miss Kensington, but first we have to get you all checked in before departure," Walker said, trying to hurry her along toward a brown door between two ticket counters. He ushered her through the door and into a small office space that had been converted into a medical exam room.

"Kindly remove all of your clothes and jewelry, Miss Kensington, and Dr. Foley will be in to see you straightaway," Walker said rapidly and nervously before quickly closing the door and locking it from the outside.

"Hey wait!" Victoria yelled and pounded on the door. She jiggled the knob, but it was locked.

Great. Here we go again. People are always locking me up -- except this time I'm supposed to strip naked and there's no sign of a swim cap, life vest or a smart phone to call somebody.

Victoria thought about screaming some more and making a scene, but then she remembered her mission. She was going to have to swallow her fears and frustrations. She would have to play the game their way -- at least until she got to where she needed to be to make her move. They would no doubt have some unpleasant surprises in store for her, but Victoria Kensington would be an actress. She would handle all of those situations with the grace of a queen until it was her turn to spring a few surprises of her own.

Victoria kicked off her 4-inch heels and then removed all of her clothes, her purple watch and all of her GPS-traceable jewelry. She set them on a chair and plopped her naked butt on the tissue paper that lined the long exam table. Then she heard a knock at the door.

"It's Dr. Foley," a man's voice said.

"Come in," Victoria said as nice as could be, though she had to work hard internally to suppress her rage at having to be seen naked by a complete stranger who may not even be a real doctor.

"Hi, Miss Kensington, I'm Dr. Myles Foley," he said, shaking her hand with a clammy palm. He smelled of cigarette smoke -- ironic for a supposed medical professional -- had bushy brown hair, a mustache, glasses, stained teeth and wore a white coat over tan slacks and brown shoes.

Dr. Foley's creepy brown eyes probed her face first, then lowered to the arms she crossed over her chest, and finally settled on her exposed private area. After the extremely awkward pause to take her all in, Dr. Foley approached her and asked her to lie back on the exam table. She reluctantly complied while still covering her breasts with her hands.

Dr. Foley put plastic gloves on his hands and wasted no time completing the main task for this exam -- probing her vagina to make sure she was still a virgin. She bit her lip, kept silent and somehow resisted the overwhelming urge to kick the quack square in the face.

"Miss Kensington, you are indeed a virgin -- four out of five will have to do," Dr. Foley said, looking at her embarrassed blue eyes this time.

"What do you mean?" she asked as she sat back up on the table, covering her breasts with her right arm and her pubic area with her left hand.

"We had to eliminate one of the contestants already because she was not a virgin as required," Dr. Foley explained with a perverted grin.

"Oh," Victoria said with a disturbed look.

Wonderful. A 25 percent chance of becoming queen now instead of 20 percent.

"Can I put my clothes back on now?" she asked. "And where did they take my bags?"

Another knock on the door interrupted them.

"Come in," Dr. Foley said without hesitation as Victoria gasped in horror, blushed and recoiled on the table.

Walker and the luggage thief both entered the room, clearly enjoying an eyeful of Victoria naked.

"What the fuck?" she shouted. "Do you people have any manners or consideration?"

So much for playing along nicely, but these surprises are really starting to suck.

"We apologize, Miss Kensington, but your departure time is approaching quickly," Walker said as he opened a closet door and pulled out a hanger with a hot pink bathrobe and matching bikini.

Meanwhile, the luggage thief grabbed all of Victoria's clothes and jewelry off the chair in one swift motion and cradled them close to his chest.

Victoria jumped up from the table and tried to pry them loose, but the agile young man eluded her before she could get a firm grip on him and ducked out of the room. Dr. Foley and Walker happily grabbed the naked Victoria and restrained her. She was a split-second from shoving both of their faces into the wall, but she caught herself just in time.

No, not now! Don't get disqualified before you even get started. Be patient and put up with it. It's their game, their rules -- for now.

"This is so not cool!" was all she said in protest.

"Miss Kensington, we do apologize for this, but we have a strict protocol for this process as demanded by King Ballentine and his security team," Walker said as Victoria sat back down on the exam table and covered herself up as best she could with her hands. Dr. Foley was unashamedly leering at her now and she glared back at him until he looked away.

"What about my clothes, watch and jewelry?" she asked with wild blue eyes. Some strands of her black hair were beginning to snake out of their twist.

"We will provide you with everything you need from this point forward in the queen contest per the regulations we have been given," Walker explained as nicely as he could while handing her the clothes hanger. "Please put on this bikini and bathrobe. Then I'll escort you to the private jet ramp for departure."

"Fine," she said, trying to compose herself again.

At *least I don't have to board the plane completely naked. Thanks so much.*

Victoria slipped into the hot pink bikini and put on the bathrobe, tying the pink belt around her slim waist.

"No shoes or sandals?" she asked as they all left the exam room.

"Later," Walker said.

Dr. Foley walked in a different direction. Victoria was happy to see that creep go elsewhere. She and Walker approached a security area.

"Please step into the X-ray machine, Miss Kensington," Walker instructed her, pointing to a tall white tube.

"But you've already stripped me," she protested.

"We must make sure you don't have any tracking devices hidden within your body," Walker said.

Victoria held her tongue and obeyed, stepping into the tube and not setting it off in any way.

Walker smiled. "Now we can have you join the other three contestants on the jet," he said excitedly.

"Wonderful," Victoria said, not masking the sarcasm in her voice at all as her brain assessed her terrible situation. The game had changed already, and not in her favor.

So much for Cyr's GPS jewelry. So much for Ventana and his team. I'm all out of popcorn to throw and I haven't even left Las Vegas. They'll never track me now. It's all on me -- just as I knew it would be.

Chapter 18

Date: March 17, 2036
Place: McCarran International Airport, Las Vegas

Three beautiful young women stared at Victoria Kensington as she entered the plush main cabin of the long, sleek private jet. Flight coordinator/steward Bruce Walker motioned for her to take the empty window seat to the right of fellow raven-haired contestant Georgia Fulmer. Strawberry blonde Sandy Peck and curly brown-haired Lucy Sanchez sat in the two-seat row across and to the left of them. They all leaned across the aisle, shaking hands and pleasantly introducing themselves to one another. Apparently Jessica Meyers was the one who had lied about being a virgin and had lost her chance to be queen of the United Kingdom of America.

All four remaining contestants wore hot pink bikinis and bathrobes, mounds of makeup and lots of lipstick. The cabin smelled of hairspray and expensive perfumes. If they only knew what a waste all of that would be in a matter of hours.

127

"Now that we're all on board, it should only be a few minutes before we're in the air," a smiling Walker told the teens, who ranged in age from 17 to 19. "Would any of you like a cocktail before we take off? We don't care if you drink before we reach a comfortable cruising altitude and your tray tables can stay in the down position."

"Yes, please," Georgia said, raising her hand and grinning. "Red wine if you have it."

"We certainly do," Walker said. "And the rest of you?"

Sandy ordered a rum and coke with lime, Lucy opted for a screwdriver and Victoria joined her row-mate Georgia in ordering a red wine. It would be her second glass of the evening.

Walker fetched their drinks and delivered them in clear, hard plastic glasses before retreating behind a door toward the front of the plane. There was a bathroom on the left toward the back of the 15-foot-long main cabin and another door leading to a section in the rear of the plane. That door was locked to the contestants as Victoria found out when she tried to open it after using the small bathroom before takeoff.

Victoria returned to her seat, smiled at the lovely Georgia as Walker's voice came over the intercom. He instructed the women to fasten their seatbelts and prepare for takeoff as the cabin lights dimmed. They all complied and sipped their drinks in silence as the twin-engine jet revved its wing engines and moved into position on the runway. Victoria gazed out her window at the jet's white wing lights and the yellow runway lights piercing the dark night.

At least planes aren't that different in 2036, she thought. But this one was much smaller than the one she recalled flying to New York with her mother and brother in 1980. Her mom held her hand during takeoff because she was scared, having never flown before.

Victoria felt like Margeaux again for a minute as she fought back tears looking out the window. She missed her mother terribly at this moment. *All those years I don't get to share with her because I've been hijacked into the future. She's 89 now -- all but dead.* Margeaux felt cheated and bitter. A tear broke through and rolled down her left cheek.

Georgia watched Victoria's reflection in the window. "Are you OK?" she asked.

Victoria wiped her cheek with her hand as the jet began speeding down the runway.

"Yeah, it's nothing. I'm just afraid of flying," she said, gazing into Georgia's pretty green eyes. She had high cheek bones and a small beauty mark above her full red lips.

"Me, too," the 19-year-old Georgia said, offering her hand with a dash of warm Southern hospitality. "That's why I didn't want the window seat. Sorry."

Victoria gladly clasped Georgia's right hand with her left hand, realizing perhaps Cyr's face was not the last friendly one she would ever see. The loud, powerful jet surged off the runway and climbed into the partly cloudy, near-midnight skies above Las Vegas. Georgia leaned against Victoria's left shoulder as the plane banked sharply to the right and they both looked out the window together, gazing down on the blazing lights of the Vegas strip.

I'm the one gambling the most right now, Victoria mused. *I better come up with a damn good poker face and fast.*

Victoria reached with her right hand for the wine glass on the tray table and swallowed a big gulp.

"Thank you, Georgia," Victoria said, admiring the shiny, emerald eyes of her rival and potential new friend. "I feel better already."

"You're welcome," Georgia said with a breezy smile.

Then Victoria spoke louder and addressed all of the other women.

"So who really wants to be queen and who just wants to be on TV?" she asked with a chuckle.

The other women laughed. Sandy, 18, perked up at the prospect of some girl talk, flashing a perfect smile and lively blue eyes. Her hair was long and full of body. Her ample chest pushed her pink bikini top to its limits.

"I see this opportunity as a great adventure," she said, gesturing with both hands. "I can't wrap my head around being an actual queen, but it sure sounds interesting."

Lucy, who had a few freckles on her light-brown-skinned face, carried herself as the toughest of the four even though she was just 17, like Victoria. She spoke with a huskier voice than her petite figure would suggest and she had an edgy attractiveness about her.

"I can't believe we're down to four already," Lucy said. "I mean that Jessica girl tried to get on the show without even being a virgin. That's pretty desperate, right?"

"I can't believe they had the gall to actually check us like that," Victoria said.

"Yeah, that Dr. Foley was a total perv," Georgia said.

"I bet he wasn't even a real doctor -- just some sicko," Sandy said with an expression of disgust.

All four nodded their heads in unison.

"Do you guys have any idea where they're taking us?" Victoria asked.

"Nobody tells us anything," Lucy said. "Everything is top secret."

"I just hate that they took all of our clothes and jewelry," Victoria said.

"And then they make us dress us up like pink Playboy bunnies," Lucy said bitterly.

"What? I kind of like it," Sandy said with a smirk, not surprising the other three one bit.

They all turned quiet as Bruce Walker opened the door and stood in front of them again.

"How about a late-night dinner, ladies?" asked the seemingly harmless little man with the shifty eyes.

"Yes, I'm starved," said Lucy, the smallest of the four.

The other three also were ready to eat. Walker served them hot plates of steak with baked potato, gravy and steamed vegetables. He also provided a

second round of drinks as two flat-screen TV
monitors automatically dropped down from the
ceiling in front of their seats. Robert Ballentine's
familiar face appeared on the screen in a pre-taped
welcoming video.

"Good evening ladies and thank you for your
interest in becoming my queen in the new United
Kingdom of America," he said with his Australian
accent and brash baritone voice. "Relax, sit back
and enjoy the flight. Put my man Bruce to work and
make sure he gets you everything you desire. I will
see you all very soon. In the meantime, while you
dine, please watch this beautiful documentary about
the most famous royal couple in the world -- King
William and Queen Kate of Great Britain. That
should get you in the mood."

"Ooh, I love them," Sandy cooed as Balls
signed off and the British royal documentary began.

Victoria enjoyed her dinner and the movie. The
third glass of wine didn't hurt. She was tipsy and a
little sleepy, and the flight was surprisingly smooth
so far with almost no turbulence on this increasingly
clear, star-lit night. She also enjoyed the company
of her three rivals. It was refreshing to have some
fellow teenage companions on this crazy journey.

And yet, deep down, Victoria sensed it was all
a setup. She noticed Walker was increasingly
twitchy, edgy and uncomfortable around them --
like he knew something weird was about to happen
but he wasn't allowed to tell them. Having
absolutely no idea where they were flying or even
what direction certainly didn't help to calm
Victoria's rising nerves. She just hoped she didn't

have another seizure. She had never experienced anything like that before in her life and it frightened her to the core. She was so tired of having no control over every situation she was being thrust into -- no wonder her body was beginning to revolt. Or was it, as Cyr believed, the leap forward's ill effects? *It has to be. That's the price I have to pay, I guess, for suddenly being able to throw Navy Seals into walls.*

Victoria took another sip of wine and closed her eyes. She wanted to try to sleep while she could because she had no idea what awaited her. All four women, in fact, drifted off to sleep in their bikinis and bathrobes, but Walker didn't let them rest for very long. Victoria stirred in her sleep and barely opened her right eye to observe Walker creep back into the cabin, leer at all of them for several moments and suspiciously check his black watch. *This weirdo is definitely up to something.* She discreetly checked her wrist out of habit to see what time it was, but they had confiscated her trusty purple watch along with her GPS-traceable jewelry. She missed the watch almost as much as her mother, who had given it to her when she turned 16. Again, tears watered her eyes.

Then Walker touched a button toward the front of the cabin and the lights went from dim to bright inside the jet.

"Ladies, we've nearly reached the end of the first leg of our journey," Walker announced, doing his best to maintain the tone of a tour guide while his shifty eyes betrayed him.

Victoria did indeed feel the jet beginning to descend at a steady pace. The three other women slowly roused, yawning, stretching and fussing with their hair.

"Ladies, please move along to the rear cabin of the jet for arrival," Walker said, pointing toward the door that had been locked to Victoria earlier.

"OK, but what's wrong with these seats?" Sandy mumbled, shaking her head in a befuddled fashion. She didn't receive an answer from Walker.

Victoria and her three cohorts stood up and stretched.

"Very good, ladies, now let's follow me," Walker said, opening the rear door of the main cabin with the slide of a card key and motioning for them to go ahead of him.

Here we go again, Victoria feared. *Of course, this has to be where it all goes to shit. Another fucking door to God knows what.*

Once all four women entered the dim rear cabin, Walker did not follow and quickly closed the door behind them. Victoria watched him do it, never once looking her in the eye, but she did not put up a fight. *Their game, their rules -- for now.*

The sound of the jet's engines seemed louder in the far less cozy tail section and the four women were immediately approached by four handsome men wearing parachute gear. They all looked like clean-cut, military-type Caucasians.

"Good early morning to you ladies. I'm Vince," said the rugged lead guy with short, spiky brown hair, green eyes and a charming Australian accent. "Ben, Chuck, Marty and I will be assisting you with your arrival procedures. Please put on these wetsuits and we'll take care of the rest. We'll be handling the other equipment you need."

"Equipment for what?" Georgia asked with a crazed look.

"They expect us to jump out of the jet," Lucy deduced matter-of-factly.

Victoria paled at the thought. *What did I say about handling unpleasant surprises with the grace of a queen? Fuck that!*

"I am not doing that," she said flatly.

Sandy quickly grabbed Victoria's arm in solidarity.

"That makes two of us," she said, shaking like a leaf.

"Three of us," Georgia chimed in.

"Is it a tandem jump?" Lucy asked.

"Yes, ma'am," Vince replied.

Lucy seemed OK with that. "I've done it a couple of times -- it's actually really fun," the petite Hispanic girl told her rivals.

They all looked at her with daggers in their eyes.

"It's the middle of the goddamn night over God knows what!" Georgia shouted, her Southern hospitality clearly left behind in the main cabin.

"Are we even over land?" Victoria asked, the question itself freaking out Sandy and Georgia even more. "Of course not. Why else would we need wetsuits?"

"No," Vince said. "This will be four tandem dives into the ocean where we will be picked up by a boat that is already in the area and knows we're coming."

"No way in hell," Georgia said, quickly emerging as the loudest voice of the opposition.

"Are you people crazy?" Sandy asked, bending down and covering her eyes from the stress. "Seriously deranged?"

"And the king had the gall to tell us to sit back, relax and enjoy the flight," Victoria scoffed.

"I am truly sorry, ladies, but due to the king's security concerns, this is your only option," Vince said. "You must parachute. The jet will not be dropping you off at an airport and you cannot stay on the jet."

"Or what -- are you going to shoot us or something?" Georgia shouted at Vince.

"No, but it is our job to get you off this jet one way or the other," he replied firmly. "You can either go nicely and tandem jump with a parachute. Or we can push you out without a parachute, which will end badly for you. It's your choice."

"I'm ready to tandem dive," Lucy said, removing her pink bathrobe, and grabbing a wetsuit and goggles from Ben. She would later hook up with him as her jump leader.

Georgia and Sandy shifted their hot bodies into reverse and pounded on the locked door to the main cabin. Chuck and Marty brushed past Victoria and dragged the crying women away from the door. Ben assisted the two men with stripping the women down to their bikinis, shoving them into their wetsuits and hooking them up to their respective dive leaders, who wore parachutes on their backs.

Vince stared at Victoria. "Nicely or like that?" he asked.

Victoria recalled what she did to the much larger Ventana, but she didn't hate this stranger enough to knock him senseless. She decided to suck it up and obey for the sake of her mission.

"Nicely," she finally said.

"Then I will jump with you," Vince said.

"Where is the jet going after this?" she asked while slipping out of her bathrobe, getting into her wetsuit and strapping goggles over her head to protect her eyes.

"I am not allowed to say," he said, helping her with the zippers and then hooking her up with himself with some assistance from Marty.

"Of course you're not," Victoria said.

Moments later, four pairs of tandem jumpers edged toward the rear of the jet as Vince pulled a lever to open a hatch. Georgia and Sandy shrieked as the cold 10,000-foot night air rushed into the tail section and made the whole unexpected nightmare become far too real. Vince had to shout his commands over the din of engine noise and howling winds. Victoria was tied to the front of him so she saw everyone approach the edge for their dives.

"Go!" he yelled to Lucy and Ben. And just like that, they tumbled into the dark abyss below the plane.

"No! Please no! No! No! No!" Sandy screamed and struggled, but Chuck easily overpowered her and pushed her toward the edge.

"Go!" Vince shouted, and out they went.

Georgia made the sign of the cross as Marty heaved her to the edge.

"Go!" Vince ordered, and Georgia went flying into the night with Marty on her back.

Then Bruce Walker suddenly reappeared in front of Victoria as Vince shuffled toward the edge with his back to the opening. Apparently it was Walker's job to close the hatch after the final jump. Victoria glared at the sneaky little man as her heart raced and her body braced for a sudden free fall. She was actually relieved Vince was going to yank her out backward so she didn't have to look.

"Best of luck to you in the queen contest, Miss Kensington," Walker yelled with a twitchy smile as he grabbed the lever with his right hand.

"Screw" was the only word Victoria got to shout before Vince back-flipped them out of the jet. They tumbled, spun and plunged through the air at tremendous speed toward a chilly, wet and moon-lit date with the Pacific Ocean.

Chapter 19

Date: March 18, 2036

Place: On the road between Las Vegas and Kingsbury, Nevada

Bill Cyr's smart phone chimed during the limo ride back to Area 52. Lou Ventana's battered face appeared when Cyr picked the phone up off the floor. He must've knocked it off the seat when he keeled over to take a nap.

"Bad news," the Navy Seal told him as he massaged the stubble on his shaved head and winced. His nose and forehead were still ugly and purple from the beating Margeaux Quigley had given him, but the pain coming from inside his head hurt far more.

"More headaches from the CAR trip?" Cyr asked, rubbing the sleep out of his eyes.

"Cranium-splitting ones," Ventana confirmed.

"What's the other bad news?" Cyr asked, now sitting upright and alert.

"We never established GPS tracking on our promoted white pawn," Ventana said, referring to

Victoria Kensington. "The jewels she wore are still at the airport."

Cyr shook his head. "I guess I shouldn't be surprised," he said. "They're certainly thorough. They must've stripped the poor girl down to her birthday suit. Any word on the jet's whereabouts?"

"Ten private jets -- all the same make and model -- departed in 10 different directions all within 20 minutes of the first one taking off," Ventana reported. "We had some people tracking all 10 of them, but ..."

"But what?" Cyr asked.

"All 10 flew to various points over the Pacific Ocean and turned around," Ventana said. "They all appear to be heading back to Vegas."

Cyr pounded his right fist into his left thigh in frustration. "Any chance you think Ballentine is going to film this queen charade in Vegas?" he asked.

"Negative," Ventana said. "My best guess is they made those ladies jump."

Cyr's eyeballs popped open. "Jump? You've got to be shitting me, Lou," he said. "From a jet ... into the Pacific ... at night ... big waves ... teenage girls in dresses and heels?"

"Even if they survive the jump, they might drown getting tangled up in their parachutes as they try to fight the waves," Ventana said with no empathy in his voice.

"These people truly are crazy," Cyr said. "But they are very smart, extremely organized and always a step ahead of us at every turn. It's aggravating."

"Our promoted white pawn is our secret weapon -- she's our Trojan horse right now," Ventana pointed out.

"One seizure-prone teenage girl," Cyr said, putting his head in his hands.

"No ordinary teenage girl. They'll underestimate her and they'll pay for it," Ventana said confidently, speaking like someone with experience in that area.

"She still won't be enough," Cyr said. "Track every ship and dingy in the Pacific Ocean. They'll pluck them out of the water tonight and have them in the pirate's hands in time for Wednesday night's show."

"Like next day air and shipping," Ventana quipped with a slight grin.

"Save your jokes for when this king is dead and my stepmother is rescued, will you Lou?" Cyr pleaded.

"Yes sir," Ventana said.

Chapter 20

Date: March 18, 2036
Place: Somewhere in the eastern Pacific Ocean
Victoria Kensington's heart was nearly lodged in her throat as her wind-buffeted body spiraled and plummeted through a cloudless, moonlit sky. She had a stranger named Vince strapped above her while she stared into the mouth of an endless Pacific Ocean that rushed up to swallow her. She couldn't locate the other three pairs of jumpers. They were below her somewhere. Perhaps they had already hit the water. The thought of smacking into a cold, angry wave of salt water made her shiver uncontrollably inside her wetsuit and goggles. *This sure as hell is no time for a seizure. Get a grip!*

Fortunately, the rugged man strapped against her at least provided some body heat. When the individual white crests of the waves became more visible, Vince pulled the parachute cord and they were jerked out of their freefall within seconds. Victoria could feel the upward yank of the chute right through her torso before the wind died down considerably and they began floating toward the sea. Soon Victoria could make out three tiny lights about 100 feet below her feet. A relatively small boat with a much larger light approached the smaller lights.

"You're doing great," Vince shouted. "We're almost ready for splash down. We'll have you out of the water fast so don't worry."

What, me worry? I'm para-trooping into enemy territory with zero backup and this guy wants me to relax.

"OK," was all Victoria said as she turned her head enough to see that Vince, too, had turned on a small light on the band of his goggles so they could be spotted easily by the boat picking them up.

Finally, Victoria and Vince crashed into the ocean and plunged beneath the frigid water. Despite the wetsuit, Victoria's body felt the shock of the impact and was surprised how cold the salt water was. Vince hoisted her to the surface with his arms and they both began treading water and gasping for air as the waves tossed them about. She flipped her goggles into the sea and wiped her eyes so she could see more clearly as Vince efficiently slashed the parachute cords away from them with a small, sharp knife that he had sheathed in a utility belt around the waist of his wetsuit. Victoria licked the salt water on her lips and tasted it while lazy eight-foot swells tossed her body to and fro, up and down. *I survived the jump at least. Amazing. What didn't kill me just might make me stronger. Look out King Balls. I'm one big-ass black square closer to you now.*

"Ready to swim?" Vince asked her from behind.

"Yes," she said.

He cut the tethers between them and set Victoria free. She immediately began swimming and splashing around. It felt good to move her muscles again. It was actually a perfectly calm night on the Pacific with a banana moon and millions of stars looking down on them.

Though the sound of voices and the boat's engine spoiled the natural beauty of the moment, Victoria was more than ready to be rescued and dry off. A wave pushed her upward and she could see the boat and its spotlight approaching their position at a steady clip. Vince swam next to her, held her with his right hand and waved at the boat with his left hand.

When the boat stopped and bobbed alongside them, Victoria felt Vince pick her up with his hands around her slim waist and thrust her into the hands of Ben. He lifted her over the side of the boat and set her down in a seat next to shivering Sandy Peck. Georgia and Lucy were chattering in the two seats ahead of them. After Ben extended his hand over the side of the boat, Vince grabbed it and climbed aboard.

"Grab them some blankets before they get hypothermia," he ordered the other men. Marty ducked into the small cabin in front of the seats and re-emerged with a few orange blankets. He quickly draped them over the four wet, shivering queen contestants, who had huddled close together in pairs, as Vince gave the boat's driver a thumb's up.

The boat immediately surged forward, gained speed and carved through the waves at nearly 40 miles per hour. A large ship outlined by numerous lights appeared less than a mile away. Sandy grabbed Victoria's hand.

"Can you believe we just lived through that?" she shouted over the steady din of the engine and the intermittent crash of waves against the hull of the 22-foot boat.

"No, I can't, but we've only just begun," Victoria yelled back.

Georgia and Lucy smiled back at them despite quivering lips. *So much for perfect hair, lipstick, makeup and perfume. Now we all look, feel and smell like half-drowned sea hags,* Victoria mused.

"I told you guys it would be fun," Lucy shouted.

"I don't know if *fun* is the right word," Sandy said as the boat dipped and rolled to the right a bit while scaling a bigger wave.

"Whoa, I think I'm going to be sick," Georgia said, putting her hand over her mouth.

"Not on me! Turn the other way," Lucy ordered, leaning away from her.

Georgia managed to retain her steak dinner and the boat pulled alongside what appeared to be a massive oil barge. A ladder awaited them on the side of the barge and men were peering down at them from the deck.

"The waves are picking up so we better climb with the women on our backs," Vince instructed his men. They each leaned forward to grab a woman.

"Piggyback time, ladies," Vince told them. "Keep your blankets wrapped around you and then you wrap your arms around us."

"Great," Sandy said sarcastically as she gazed fretfully at the long ladder made of thick rope extending at least four stories up to reach the deck of the gigantic barge. And yet, after jumping out of a jet and parachuting into the ocean, this, too, seemed doable.

Again Vince and Victoria would go last. She watched intently as the three co-ed pairs slowly climbed up the sides of the ship. Then it was their turn. Vince waved to the boat driver, waited for a swell to even out and grabbed a rung of the ladder with Victoria clinging tightly to his chest and back. Vince's strong, wiry limbs jumped into action and he scaled the ladder relatively fast considering he had 120 water-logged pounds strapped to his back. Victoria frequently held her breath and never looked down as they left the water behind and made their way up to the ship's dry, grimy deck.

When they reached the top, Victoria got off Vince's back and tried to focus her eyes in the glare of the lights. She didn't get much of a chance.

"Let's go!" Vince ordered the group, grabbing her by the hand and leading her across the long, flat deck of the barge to, *oh no, another plane.*

"What the fuck?" she shouted, noticing two military-looking jets, one on each end of the former oil barge that had been converted into a mini aircraft carrier. A pair of Chinese-made, state-of-the-art, long-range stealth harrier jets were rumbling and waiting for their cargo.

146

Vince and his men made the women strip off their wetsuits and dry off their bikini-clad bodies with their orange blankets for a minute. Then the four women donned gray, full-length jet suits, masks and black boots.

Each jet could hold three occupants. The pilots were already in the front seats and waiting. Vince and his men helped two pairs of women climb into the single-file passenger seats behind the pilots. Victoria and Georgia sat second and third, respectively, in the jet on the west end of the barge while Lucy and Sandy did the same on the east-end jet.

Moments later, Victoria's jump jet powered its engines to full throttle and took off vertically from the big white X on the dark brown deck of the barge. When it reached an altitude of a few hundred feet, the jet blasted forward and began to climb far more rapidly than the other jets she had flown. *Holy shit!*

Victoria practically hyperventilated in her oxygen mask as the forces of the jet groped and tugged at her body. She felt light-headed and again worried about having a seizure, but the jet quickly leveled off and the pilot's strange voice in her ear speaker shook her out of that scary train of thought.

"Welcome aboard," he said with an unmistakable Chinese accent. "We are already at our extremely low cruising altitude of 8,000 feet to help avoid radar detection. Enjoy the flight, ladies. It's a beautiful night to fly."

Yeah, it's a beautiful night to be strip-searched, fly a little, get pushed out of a jet, get dumped into the ocean and fly all over again. Very relaxing. I want to kill Balls just for making me do all of this -- never mind everything else he's done!

"Are we going to have to jump out of this jet, too?" Victoria heard Georgia ask the pilot. She understandably sounded frazzled to the point of tears.

"Negative," the pilot assured her.

"Thank you, God and Jesus," Georgia said with relief.

"That is wonderful news," Victoria said, "but can you tell us where we're flying to now?"

"Negative. Very sorry," the pilot replied.

"What a surprise," Victoria said bitterly.

The two harrier jets flew for several hours at low altitude and high speed until they reached their destination -- a Chinese aircraft carrier named Invincible about 125 miles south-southwest of Wake Island in the western Pacific Ocean. After landing on the massive ship, the four groggy, jet-lagged women were quickly whisked into a black helicopter and flown south as the sun rose in the east.

Victoria cupped her hand around her right eye to avoid the sun's glare, which was beginning to give her a migraine. She could only see many more endless miles of sea out the right window of the chopper. The other three women had quickly fallen back to sleep despite the raucous drone and unsettling vibrations of the helicopter. The four women sat two-by-two in the four-seat compartment behind the spiky-haired Chinese pilot.

This time Lucy was to the left of Victoria while Georgia and Sandy slumped behind them.

I am so over this, Victoria thought. *A few more minutes and I might jump out of this thing just to put me out of my misery. The president can rescue herself. Or Ventana can. I had no idea I would be dragged halfway around the world like a piece of luggage -- without my own luggage! I can't believe these three crazy teens with me actually want to be this maniac's queen ... lover ... disgusting!*

Just as she winced at that thought and her own seemingly suicidal mission to deceive this so-called monarch, Victoria's gut churned harder than her head ached. Her weary blue eyes caught sight of a long, beautiful white yacht about a half mile away and a few hundred feet below the helicopter. It dazzled like a mirage on the shimmering sea.

That's got to be him. A boat suitable for a filthy rich corporate pirate out in the middle of absolutely nowhere. Now this gets very real and I'm in deep.

The chopper banked hard to the right. Victoria saw more waves rippling below her as the yacht seemingly pulled her closer like an unrelenting current.

Within two minutes, the helicopter hovered above the sky deck helipad of the spectacular 253-foot yacht named "Rendezvous Two." The other women began to stir in their seats as Victoria glimpsed three men loitering near the landing pad below to receive the four would-be queens. Once again, Victoria's heart raced in her chest and adrenaline coursed through her body. Her mind, too, switched on.

Wake up and stay sharp. I'm Victoria Kensington from Newport, Rhode Island. ... I'm Victoria Kensington from Newport, Rhode Island ... not whoever I was before. This is show time. Game on.

Chapter 21

Date: March 18, 2036

Place: Aboard the yacht "Rendezvous Two" in the western Pacific Ocean

As the Chinese pilot deftly lowered the black helicopter onto the helipad of the Rendezvous Two, Victoria Kensington and her three rivals were all relieved to be done with air travel. After surviving a private jet and parachute jump, motor boat and oil barge, harrier jet and helicopter ride, the young women had now landed in a floating lap of luxury.

"A yacht will certainly do," Sandy Peck quipped as she tried to fluff up her now lifeless hair. Georgia Fulmer and Lucy Sanchez also began to perk up after sleeping for nearly the entire helicopter flight since taking off from the Chinese aircraft carrier Invincible. All four women were still wearing their gray, full-length jet suits and black boots they had put on way back at the oil barge.

From her helicopter window, Victoria spied an elevated Jacuzzi, white cabana beds and lounge chairs toward the bow of the four-level ship's sky deck. The sleek yacht aimed west like an arrowhead toward an endless blue horizon. Outside Lucy's window, Victoria observed the dark-tinted windows of the captain's wheelhouse looming over the helipad and sky deck.

When the helicopter landed smoothly and the pilot turned off the engine, two crew members dressed in white polo shirts, khaki shorts and brown sandals helped the women exit the chopper. The queen contestants were guided away from the whirling rotors and toward some white lounge chairs that lined the sand-colored, wooden sky deck. Another man -- wearing a Hawaiian shirt, khaki shorts, a brown belt holstering a slew of high-tech gadgets, and beige sandals -- walked ahead and motioned for them to stretch out on the lounge chairs. The women, with their hair blowing all around their faces from the helicopter and the Pacific Ocean breezes, quickly complied and waited for further instructions while the noise from the chopper died down. Moments later, the 30-something, 5-foot-10, 175-pound man with short brown hair and glasses began talking and acting like their tour guide.

"Hello ladies and welcome to the Rendezvous Two," the man said with sincere-looking hazel eyes, hospitable charm and, of course, an Australian accent. "My name is Howard Nelson. I am a media specialist for King Robert Ballentine and I will also be your go-to person aboard ship for anything you need. I will give you a tour of the Rendezvous Two later. She is a magnificent yacht. But first, we will escort you to your private cabins on the second deck so you can get some much-needed sleep."

"Thank you!" Georgia exulted with both hands clasped, eliciting smiles all around.

"You're welcome," Nelson said empathetically. "The king and I do apologize for making you suffer so much to get here, but staging this contest opens us up to considerable risk."

And a hostile takeover of America doesn't? Victoria mused.

Nelson checked his watch. "It is nearly 6 a.m. now, so sleep until noon, get freshened up in your private baths and we'll bring you back up to the sky deck for a 12:30 p.m. brunch. Then the king will stop by and chat with you. He's asleep right now, but he knows you've been through a terrible ordeal over the last several hours and he's left you all a considerable sum of cash under your pillows -- far more than the tooth fairy could afford. So take comfort in that at least, ladies, and go get some well-deserved beauty sleep," he said.

After a quick ride down a glass elevator from the sky deck to the second deck, a tall, handsome, blond crew member led Victoria to a door just down the hall from where Georgia, Sandy and Lucy were entering their cabins. He slid his card key into the lock, opened the door for Victoria and said, "My name is Greg. Just press 9 on the touch screen if you need anything, Miss Kensington. You'll find refreshments, fresh fruit, yogurt and other snacks in your small refrigerator to hold you over until brunch. There are plenty of dresses and bathing suits in your closet. You'll also find underclothes in the dresser. Wear whatever you like."

"How do you know they'll fit?" she asked.

"You sent us your measurements in your email," Greg replied with a warm smile and gentle blue eyes.

"Oh … oh yes, that's right," Victoria said, kicking herself internally. *I'm sure Ventana enjoyed doing that. And what did he measure me with -- his creepy eyeballs?*

"I'm sure you're exhausted from your trip, Miss Kensington. Sleep well," Greg said, closing the door.

"Yes, thank you, Greg," she said as he departed.

For once, Victoria didn't mind a door closing behind her. She would not be checking to see if it was locked. She would not be pounding at it with her fist. She stretched her hands above her weary head, yawned and glanced around her cozy square-shaped cabin. There was a small bathroom and shower off to the immediate left. Along the left wall, there was a queen-sized bed, fittingly, with a black envelope (*even his envelopes are black? really?*) protruding from beneath one of the two green pillows. There were green, tropical-patterned sheets under an orange bed spread. The cabin's walls were Paris green with white trim. The far wall was interrupted by an oversized rectangular window that looked out to the Pacific. In the far right corner opposite the bed, there was a comfortable orange chair. Along the right wall, she observed a flat-screen TV, small fridge, black dresser and closet.

Victoria happily removed her annoying black boots and jet suit, stripping down to the pink bikini Bruce Walker issued her way back at the airport in

Las Vegas. That seemed like days ago now. She
opened the closet door and found dozens of hangars
full of evening gowns, shirts, shorts and, yes, more
bikinis. Every color of the rainbow was represented
and then some. The drawers of the dresser, too,
were stuffed with everything from colorful thongs
and panties to white bras and silky pajamas. In the
teal-tiled bathroom, a full range of lipstick, makeup
and toiletries were neatly organized on a vertical
shelf unit next to the mirror and sink. The white
bath tub featured a high, oversized shower head.

Though the shower looked appealing, Victoria
was simply too tired. She shed her pink bikini,
donned some blue panties and white, silky pajamas,
brushed her teeth, used the toilet and finally crawled
onto the bed toward the black envelope. It lay under
a pillow case adorned with pineapples and coconuts
against a light green background. Victoria moved
the orange blanket aside, slipped under the sheets
and opened the envelope. She found a note,
handwritten in black ink on white paper, folded
around a wad of hundred dollar bills. It read:

Dear Miss Kensington,
Welcome aboard the Rendezvous Two. I'm so
glad you are here to be my queen. I look forward to
getting to know you straightaway. I am sure we will
hit it off well and I will see you soon during brunch
on the sky deck. Enclosed you will find my first
attempt to apologize for the hell I put you through
to reach me. Unfortunately, I am currently the most
hunted man in the world, so drastic means were
necessary to bring you aboard without any

155

*undesirable company tailing along after you. I do
hope you can understand and I promise I will
continue to make it up to you very soon. Sweet
dreams.*

*Love,
King Robert Ballentine*

Gross! Victoria thought, as she stuck out her
tongue and made a face. She didn't have to pretend
when she was alone. *Then again, what if they have
hidden cameras in here? They better not.* She began
to glance around the room, but her eyes desperately
wanted to shut. She forced them to stay open a little
longer so she could count the cash.

Victoria removed the rubber band and slapped
down 100 $100 bills on the bed -- *that's $10,000!*
She was mildly surprised to see 100 Benjamin
Franklins staring back at her. *What, no time to
change the currency yet, Balls?* She imagined the
pony-tailed pirate's head on the bill instead of Ben.
Then she tried to picture what her own face would
look like on the bill. *The old Margeaux or the
young Margeaux? Or this new me? Who the hell am
I again?*

"I'm Victoria Kensington from Newport,
Rhode Island," she told herself out loud. "I'm a 17-
year-old virgin who wants to be queen of the new
United Kingdom of America. The date is March 18,
2036."

Victoria nodded as if to reconfirm her new
identity and mission, then laid her head on the
pillow. That's when another pertinent wave of
thoughts crashed her attempt to sleep. *Where is*

President Quigley? The older me is here somewhere on this ship. I have to talk to her ... me. What will I say? How will I let her know I'm here to rescue her? ... me? ... will I even get the chance to kill Ballentine? ... Can I go through with it if I do get the chance? ... Will I get off this ship alive?

Moments later, Victoria's thoughts finally ebbed, a $100 bill fell out of her hand and sleep took over as the Rendezvous Two knifed gracefully through the ocean beneath her.

Chapter 22

Date: March 18, 2036

Place: Aboard the Rendezvous Two in the western Pacific Ocean

Freshly showered and invigorated by six hours of deep sleep, Victoria Kensington joined Howard Nelson, Sandy Peck, Lucy Sanchez and Georgia Fulmer in the glass elevator. All of the young women looked sexy in skimpy bikinis and sandals with lively hair, long eyelashes and lots of makeup. The elevator smelled like a flower garden of perfumes and Ballentine's flak, Nelson, beamed with delight at being surrounded in close quarters by such unspoiled, radiant beauty.

Amazing what a little sleep and 10 grand under our pillows can do for us, Victoria thought.

Sandy squeezed her curves into hot pink (*again? you'd think she'd be sick of that color after the private jet experience and everything after it -- not exactly good luck*); Georgia rocked the white with black polka dots; Lucy lit up in neon light green, and Victoria, after four attempts to figure out what to wear, blazed in a sleek, fire-engine red bikini with no straps and plenty of cleavage showing. There was no sense in being anything but bold, especially when she knew Ventana already had advertised her to the king as a teen vixen. It was time to act the part whether she liked it or not.

Victoria let her fine black hair cascade over her shoulders. She also made sure her already long eyelashes were fully extended and extra black -- that color, after all, was clearly the king's favorite. She refused to wear a black bikini, however. She didn't want to fry like an egg under the Pacific sun.

"The first or lowest deck of the ship has the engine rooms and sleep cabins for the crew and the king's security personnel," Nelson explained in the elevator as he pushed the number 3 and it began its short, smooth ascent to the third deck. "The second deck, as you have seen, has cabins for the king's special guests."

The glass elevator stopped at the third deck and Nelson, wearing a different Hawaiian shirt, white shorts and brown sandals, motioned for them to follow him.

"This is the third deck or waterfall deck as you will soon see why," he said, leading the women into a wide, sprawling banquet room with large rectangular windows on both sides; long, flowing black curtains; black-and-white chessboard carpeting leading toward a hardwood dance floor, and a disco ball sparkling above it in the midday sun. There were two doors beyond the dance floor that led to the open part of the waterfall deck.

In the foreground, there were several black, semicircular gaming tables with green felt surfaces and plush red stools. Along the right wall, a long cherry-wood bar appeared to be stocked with every liquor bottle known to man. Victoria observed camera equipment along the left wall and what looked like a small editing room with TV monitors in the near left corner.

"This is amazing," Victoria said, not having to act to sound enthusiastic this time.

"I love it," Sandy chimed in as the group tour headed toward the dance floor, which had a DJ booth in the far left corner and small black speakers elevated on the walls surrounding it.

"We'll be filming the show in this lounge," Nelson said. "We'll tape the semifinals tonight at 8, but the United Kingdom of America won't see it until Wednesday at 10 p.m. New York time. I can't tell you where we are, but I can say that we are eight hours behind New York time. As a result, Thursday's live finale show will be filmed at 2 p.m. our time."

"It'll be really bright in here for that -- kind of like it is now," Lucy pointed out.

"No, we'll draw all the curtains and make it seem like night just as it will be in America when they view the show," Nelson said.

Lucy gyrated her mostly naked, tanned body on the dance floor and smiled. Nelson paused to appreciate the view.

"Imagine what you could do when you're given a few cocktails and some music," Nelson said with a grin.

"I'll blow the king's mind," Lucy said, shaking her hips and ass.

"I bet you will," Nelson said, motioning the women toward one of the doors to daylight. "Let's show you the rest of the waterfall deck, shall we?"

Victoria emerged last through the door and saw a huge rectangular swimming pool lined with white lounge chairs, white tables and cabana beds on both sides. A beautiful waterfall cascaded into the pool from the elevated bow of the ship. Steps rose on the right side of the waterfall to a smaller infinity pool on the bow.

Nelson led the women through the waterfall deck and up the white steps to the sand-colored platform surrounding the infinity pool. Sandy knelt down, ran her hand through the warm water and smiled. The other women leaned against the rail and gazed out to the infinite horizon of light blue sky meeting dark blue water. The sun was blazing overhead in a cloudless sky.

Victoria squinted back toward the ship and saw how the infinity pool dropped off into seemingly nowhere, when actually the waterfall, not visible from the elevated level, took the water down into the main pool. All in all, it was a gorgeous way to travel and relax.

Too bad I'm not here on vacation. No, I'm here to pretend I want to be queen and then find a way to kill the most hunted man in the world. I'm here to rescue the president somehow. Where is President Quigley? I have to find her.

"This truly is a magnificent ship," she heard herself say to Nelson out loud. "But your tour seems incomplete. Where are the hostages kept?"

Nelson's jaw dropped open. The other women exchanged annoyed glances. *Oops. Did I really say that out loud? I'm losing it already.*

"Excuse me, Miss Kensington?" Nelson fired back, his face contorting from congenial tour guide into guarded flak in an instant.

Victoria pressed ahead as innocent-faced as she could. *Be an actress! I'm a harmless virgin from half way across the world. I watched Balls interview the president on the UKA network like millions of others. It was a ballsy but honest question.*

"I saw the king interview President Quigley on the UKA network in January and I was just curious if you let her sleep on our deck as one of the king's honored guests or on the first deck with the crew and the engine noise?" Victoria asked Nelson with an exaggerated shoulder shrug and a bat of her eyelashes.

Victoria's tough-as-nails question appeared to be giving Nelson indigestion. His mouth froze in a frown and he seemed at a loss for words in that awkward moment as the yacht dipped more than usual in front of a larger wave, then rocked upward, forcing all five of them to adjust their sandal-clad feet. A sea gull hovered and squawked overhead. Finally, he thought of something to say.

"I will make sure to tell the king of your interest in President Quigley's whereabouts and perhaps he'll discuss that with you at a later time," Nelson said smugly, recovering rather effectively.

His answer gave Victoria a feeling of indigestion and she hadn't even had brunch yet. *Shit! I'm in big trouble already.*

"Sure," was all she managed to say, hiding her unease as best she could.

Nelson quickly changed the subject as he marched back down the steps beside the waterfall and waved for them to follow him. "Come this way, ladies, and we'll head to brunch on the sky deck above us," he said, quickly back in tour-guide mode. "After brunch, the king will stop by to join you for a dip in the Jacuzzi. He knows he has a lot to learn about each of you before we start taping the semifinals tonight."

Victoria let the other women proceed ahead of her down the steps. Georgia went last and was the only one of the three to look Victoria in the eyes as she went by.

"Be careful, girl," Georgia whispered discreetly as she clutched Victoria's left wrist with her right hand. "You don't want to end up out there," she added with a nod over the rail toward the deep waters of the Pacific.

Georgia's sideways nod reminded Victoria of a soccer player heading the ball toward the goal.

Too bad I almost headed the ball into my own net. I need to be all the way down the other end of the field -- that's how far I am from where I need to be on this mission.

Then she had another thought that gave her an ocean spray of hope.

"At least I'm very, very warm," she whispered to herself as she slowly descended the steps beside the tranquil waterfall and trailed the others across the third deck. "Howard Nelson has no poker face. The president is absolutely somewhere on this ship."

Chapter 23

Date: March 18, 2036
Place: Aboard the Rendezvous Two in the western Pacific Ocean

After thoroughly enjoying a brunch of eggs, sausage, toast, bacon, pancakes, hash browns, fresh tropical fruits and coffee, the four would-be queens eased into the hot, bubbly Jacuzzi on the bow of the yacht's breathtaking sky deck. The Pacific breezes caressed their nubile faces and shoulders while the jet-propelled water massaged their backs and legs in the eight-person, circular tub. Howard Nelson had left them to chat amongst themselves before King Robert Ballentine made his grand entrance.

Nelson's going to rat me out, Victoria feared. *Me and my big mouth. He'll tell Balls I asked where they're keeping the president.* She shivered at the thought of being dumped overboard and watching the ship leave her in its wake. *Hopefully, I won't survive the fall. It's definitely a long way down. I don't want to be alive when I'm eaten by the sharks.*

Just as Victoria's brain was sealing her own fate, the most hunted man in the world arrived on the sky deck flanked by two formidable bodyguards dressed in black polo shirts, tan shorts and black sneakers. They were both the size of Ventana and armed with holstered pistols. They eyed the women like bad asses before Ballentine waved them away to go sit at a brunch table near the helipad. The helicopter was no longer there.

Victoria stared at Ballentine as he swaggered slowly up the steps to the elevated Jacuzzi area on the bow. His long, salt-and-pepper hair was pulled back tightly into his trademark ponytail. Sweat glistened on the brow over his bushy eyebrows, which weren't quite thick enough to hide his dancing blue eyes as he approached his potential queens. His mustache and goatee weren't quite thick enough to hide his smiling mouth either. Though he was 20 or so pounds overweight on a 6-foot frame, he still seemed reasonably well put together under a white silk shirt with a black logo on it, white-and-black pinstriped shorts with a black belt, hairy legs and brown sandals under his large feet. He mounted the steps and loomed above the women with a confident, amused expression. The view clearly satisfied him as he paused a moment for dramatic effect. His gold crown was not on top of his head at this particular moment, but his swollen ego seemed to make up for it.

"Good afternoon ladies," he said brightly. "I am King Robert Ballentine, but feel free to call me Rob, Robby, Bob, Bobby, Balls or whatever you like. Welcome to the Rendezvous Two -- a floating paradise, wouldn't you agree?"

"Absolutely paradise," Sandy said, quickly sucking up to him as she splashed water over her arms and heaving chest.

"I love it!" Lucy said with a sexy grin before dipping her head under water, coming up again quickly and smoothing out her brown hair as her small, perky bosom pressed together for the king's benefit. He didn't fail to notice.

"I'm glad you all survived the magic carpet ride to get here," Ballentine said with a chuckle.

"Thanks for the cash," Georgia said, licking her wet, luscious red lips and fawning at the king. "Where's your bathing suit? Aren't you coming in?"

Ballentine beamed at Georgia, locked eyes with Victoria for an awkward second (*shit, what do I say?*) and sat down on the edge of a white cabana bed beside the hot tub. He leaned forward and savored all of their beauty for a moment.

"I will … later," he said. "First, I want to watch you splash around together a little bit and see what you're like. Then I'll take a stroll with each of you one-on-one so I can get to know you personally a little better. It's going to be a whirlwind three days, but I do plan to make one of you my queen on Thursday night. Do you all feel ready for that?"

Victoria saw the opening and jumped at it.

"I've been ready since the second you selected me as a finalist, King Ballentine," she said, gliding across the Jacuzzi in a couple of smooth strokes to be closer to where he sat. She made sure her cleavage trapped his eyes. The other three women were visibly surprised at Victoria's sudden switch to offense in pursuit of the throne. If they only knew her real motive. "May I walk with you first?"

So much for watching them all splash around together. Ballentine gazed into Victoria's alluring blue eyes and couldn't refuse. He was too intrigued, too infatuated, too curious -- she really did look like a young President Quigley. The king stood right up and offered his hand to the collective gasp of Victoria's rivals.

"I'm very impressed with your initiative, Miss Kensington. Let's do that," Balls said as he helped her out of the Jacuzzi, escorted her down the steps and left the other three women behind without even looking back. They were pissed.

As the hot sun began drying her dripping wet, mostly naked body, Victoria clutched the king's left arm and pretended she was already queen. The bodyguards warily watched them stroll near the railing and toward a passage way, which extended from the right front base of the wheelhouse all the way to the stern.

"Stay where you are and give us some time alone," Ballentine ordered his men, who nodded.

The king quietly led her half way between the bow and stern of the 253-foot-long ship before stopping to look out over the Pacific. The railing came up to Victoria's chest as she rigidly gazed out toward the blue horizon. She refused to let her eyes look down at the water as frantic thoughts raced through her brain. *Is this the golden opportunity Cyr talked about? Should I hurl him overboard now?*

No, Cyr told me to be patient and 150 percent sure. I'm not sure of anything right now. Or is Balls about to hurl me overboard after what I asked Nelson? If I'm going over, he's coming with me. That's for damn sure.

Balls' baritone voice interrupted her thoughts.

"So Victoria Kensington from Newport, Rhode Island, what do you think of my yacht? You come from a place where yachting is all the rage. Newport used to host the America's Cup races just before I was born in 1984," Ballentine said, alternately studying Victoria's suddenly shy eyes and admiring the curves of her young, athletic body.

1984? What the hell? I was 17 in 1984 just a few days ago, Victoria thought. *Focus, focus!*

"I love your yacht," she said, looking up at him. With bare feet, she was 4 inches shorter than Ballentine. "My father was really into all of that, but he turned out to be an asshole. So I think I steered clear of the whole yachting thing out of spite."

Balls laughed. "That makes sense. I hope I don't remind you of him."

"No, not at all," Victoria lied. *You're a whole new category of asshole. ... Careful!*

"Victoria Kensington … what an interesting name," Balls said, almost scrutinizing every syllable of her alias as they rolled across his tongue. The hint of disbelief in his voice immediately alarmed Victoria.

"Do you like my name, king?" she asked, trying to stay calm while her heart pounded in her chest.

"Why yes, Queen Victoria does have a nice ring to it," he said, seemingly half distracted by another thought. "Tell me something, Miss Kensington. Are you and President Quigley related by any chance? It's my understanding she doesn't have any granddaughters, but you could certainly pass for one."

His tone was still cordial, but Victoria knew she was already on the spot. The wrong choice of words here could send her to a watery grave.

"No king, that's not possible," Victoria said, looking right into his probing blue eyes. "I've never met the president before in my life, though I do realize the resemblance is striking."

"Downright eerie might be a better way to put it," Balls said with a mischievous grin. He obviously enjoyed toying with the mysterious girl. "And would you really have sex with me on live TV? Let's face it, not too many virgins aspire to be porn actresses, Miss Kensington."

Ventana continues to haunt me with his slutty texts! Victoria felt cornered, queasy and light-headed. She closed her eyes for a moment and suddenly had an out-of-body experience. She was further down the railing toward the stern. She could see Ballentine's back as he was questioning her about 20 feet away. She began to move toward Balls and herself. It all looked so real. *What the hell is happening to me?*

"Are you feeling OK, Miss Kensington?" Balls asked, then glanced back over his left shoulder quickly as if he saw someone. "Who's there? What …?"

170

Just like that, Victoria was back in her body and rubbing her eyes.

"That's bizarre. Miss Kensington, did you happen to see someone behind me just now?" Balls asked with a rare befuddled expression on his face. Clearly, he didn't like surprises.

"No ... no, I didn't," Victoria said.

Ballentine looked over his shoulder again, saw nobody, rubbed his own eyes and shook his head.

"I'm sorry, king," Victoria said. "I do apologize for not feeling 100 percent at the moment."

"I totally understand, Miss Kensington, after the hellish journey I put you through," Balls said, softening his tone. "Do you want to return to your cabin and get more sleep?"

"Absolutely not," Victoria said, quickly gathering herself and refocusing on her mission. "I am young and I am strong. I will fight off this jet lag and have sex with you right here and now if you want. I don't need to wait for the TV show."

Ballentine smiled broadly at that bold and unexpected response. He impulsively kissed her on the lips. *Gross! He better not call my bluff,* Victoria feared.

"As tempted as I am, I will have to defer for now," he said, seemingly surprised and delighted that Victoria matched how forward she was in her email application. "I want to give all four of you an equal chance to be queen. Having sex with you will affect my decision."

Relieved by his answer and emboldened by her new tack, Victoria laughed as sexily as she could while grabbing his right arm with both hands. "Correction, king. It would've ended the contest before it started," she said lustily, then kissed his neck -- ironically, the same neck she wanted to strangle. *That's better. Act, act, act!*

Balls blinked a few times, smiled and nodded. He almost seemed wobbly for a second. The sudden twists and turns with this strange young woman already were having an effect. *Practically a knockout with just a few words,* Victoria's brain cheered. *Perhaps we've struck upon a weakness here. He is human after all. Stay on the offensive.*

"Why did you want to become king? Is it the love of power?" Victoria asked, putting the questions to him this time. The innocent curiosity in her voice proved nearly as seductive as the kiss on his neck.

Balls blushed, pondered her question for a moment and smiled. He wasn't used to being interviewed. He preferred to be the interviewer.

"Yes, I love power," he said, gazing into her eyes. "I love waking up in the morning knowing I'm the man in charge. I love taking risks and seeing where they get me. Taking on a queen is a major risk, but I've always been a gambler."

"Come on. Do I really look that risky to you?" Victoria asked playfully.

"You are, without a doubt, the riskiest of the four women I will choose from," he replied with a tone more serious than she expected. "And that's why I want you to be my queen."

Chapter 24

Date: March 19, 2036
Place: Area 52, Kingsbury, Nevada
Bill Cyr invited Jimmy Baker and G52 to the
L-shaped room to watch Wednesday night's queen
semifinals show on the UKA network. Lou Ventana
and his Navy Seal team were already en route to
one of five areas of the Pacific they had projected
Ballentine's ship could be based on the flight
patterns of the 10 private jets. It was a shot in the
dark, but they were tired of waiting around and
doing nothing in the underground bunker.
Unfortunately for Ventana and his fellow Seals,
who were traveling aboard a converted fishing
vessel to escape detection, they were stalking a
cruise ship traveling along the Alaskan coast. In
short, they were very, very cold.

Cyr and Baker shared a bowl of popcorn in the
viewing room as G52 rolled in between their two
chairs with all four of his green digital eyes atwitter.

"I can't wait to see Margeaux," Bake said
excitedly, wearing a gold Lake Tahoe cap Cyr had

given him, a green-and-white-striped golf shirt, blue jeans and white sneakers.

"I just hope she made it to his ship OK and she remembers her alias is Victoria Kensington," Cyr said, the stress making his tired eyes sag.

"Still no success tracking source of the UKA signal," G52 reported through his automated translator speaker. "Chinese are using some new method to filter original signal and bounce it out in hundreds of different directions. One tentacle of the signal originates from Los Angeles, California, in a section called Hollywood."

"They do have a sense of humor," Cyr said disgustedly.

"I will try to reach mission target telepathically," G52 said.

"Do you think you can?" Cyr asked with wide eyes and a glimmer of hope.

"I know I can do this," the alien said. "The question is, will young woman understand message on her end?"

"Can you guys keep it down, the show is about to start," Bake implored them. "You wouldn't have any beer to wash down this popcorn, would ya?"

Cyr glared at the young man for a second before pausing to fondly recall a beer-bonding experience between himself and his late father many years ago when he was a teen.

"Of course Jimmy," Cyr said with a smile. "Grab one from the small fridge in the conference room."

"Thanks Bill," the teen said with a grin. He fetched a beer and returned in no time at all. "Hey, did you guys want one? I should've asked. Maybe some plant matter and sulfur for 52 here?"

"No thanks, Jimmy. We're fine," Cyr said with a chuckle.

Ballentine's face appeared on the big flat screen TV in front of them with his usual classical music introduction. Then an Australian-sounding narrator's voice introduced the four queen finalists as both still and video images of them flashed on the screen. Victoria looked alive, healthy and beautiful, much to Cyr's relief, but he noticed something was already amiss.

"Only four women?" Cyr blurted out between mouthfuls of popcorn. "I thought there were five vying for the crown."

"Maybe one was too ugly for King Balls," Bake guffawed before chugging some beer.

"Don't drink that too fast," Cyr nagged him. "You've got a two-drink maximum, Jimmy. You've already had a couple of headaches from the CAR trip as it is."

"You make a good point, Bill," Bake said, taking a smaller sip this time.

The Australian-sounding host -- who had brown hair and glasses, and wore a gray suit and light blue tie -- then explained to the camera why Ballentine had only four women in the running to be his queen.

"Jessica Meyers was disqualified because she was not, in fact, a virgin per our rules," the man said matter-of-factly.

"Wow, these guys actually checked -- that's pretty …," Bake said.

"Thorough," Cyr interrupted him.

"Radically messed up, yet fascinating, I was going to say, Bill," Bake concluded with a grin and another half-chug of beer.

The Australian host went on to explain that King Ballentine would hand out roses to two of the four women at the end of the one-hour show. Then Balls would select his queen in a live finale Thursday night at 10 Eastern Standard Time.

"That's 7 p.m. our time," Cyr noted.

"Different time, only channel," Bake quipped, referring to Ballentine's complete domination of all major cable network signals with his UKA network.

The next segment of the show featured the host interviewing each of the four women separately so they could talk about themselves and why they wanted to be queen. They all wore long, fancy evening gowns with diamond earrings, necklaces and bracelets. Victoria looked stunning in dark blue with her hair up. Her blue eyes dazzled as much as the jewels, none of which were GPS-traceable, Cyr lamented. Victoria sold her story well and spoke confidently.

"That girl may get an Oscar yet for her performance," Cyr said with more than a hint of pride in his voice.

"She'll also win hands down," Bake added. "Georgia is pretty hot, too, but Margeaux ... I mean, Victoria ... come on, man. Balls will definitely pick her. Then what? She puts a little arsenic in the king's steak sauce or what?"

"Don't worry about that, Jimmy -- you don't need to lose sleep over it, too," Cyr said.

Ballentine dined with all four women in some dark, candlelit lounge and chatted personably with each of them in turn. Again, Victoria held her own with His Radiance, Cyr observed. She smiled warmly, carried herself with polish and grace well above her 17 years, and even made Balls laugh on a couple of occasions.

"Yeah, he totally wants her," Bake deduced with a snort. "He looks at Margeaux the most and talks to her way more than the other chicks. Lucy is weird and Sandy is a total ditz."

Cyr smiled. He sorely needed some comic relief and this buzzed teen with the unfiltered sense of humor provided that in spades. G52, on the other hand, was a font of silence.

"Any thoughts?" Cyr asked the alien.

"Threat level to our mission target is extremely high," the alien said.

"Our mission target is now Robert Ballentine, not Margeaux Quigley-17. Do you understand, 52?" Cyr asked.

"Yes," 52 replied.

"Then what's your assessment?" Cyr persisted.

"Threat levels to black king and white pawn-promoted-to-white queen both extremely high," 52 said. "This match could go either way based on present positions."

"That's not very enlightening 52, but I do appreciate the chess metaphor," Cyr said with an uneasy grin.

Then the TV show took a turn for the bizarre. Ballentine's version of dinner and dancing apparently required the four women to perform all around him at the same time on the dance floor while he sat perched upon an elevated throne with his black suit, pony tail and golden crown. In this segment of the obviously pre-taped show, the women all wore short, revealing black cocktail dresses and black heels. A song by 1990s-era band Nine Inch Nails pulsed from the speakers as the women gyrated and seduced their king.

"Bow down before the one you serve, you're going to get what you deserve," the male singer's voice growled over a vicious, hooky, goth-industrial beat.

Bake's jaw dropped open and some beer drool fell from his gaping mouth as he watched his classmate and her three rivals shake and shimmy their assets like nothing he had ever seen before.

"I guess queens are wild tonight," Cyr quipped. "And believe it or not, Jimmy, I do remember that song from my younger days. The king is only looping the part he likes. He's leaving out another important lyric -- 'I'd rather die than give you control.'"

"I've never heard that song in my life," Bake said in a zombie-like state, his eyes still fixed on the TV screen. "I like it … I like it … make that I'm in love with it now."

"I can see why," Cyr said. "I also know why you've never heard the song -- you're from 1984 and 'Head Like a Hole' came out in the 1990s."

"That would make sense," Bake said, nodding as Victoria bowed to the beat beneath leering King Ballentine on the TV screen. "Who knew I'm so behind the times?"

After the tribal dance number and several more clips of the four women talking to the camera, Ballentine answered a few questions from the host. Then there was a tease to the rose ceremony followed by several minutes of commercials.

"Boy, they're really milking this," Bake said.

Finally, the shameless egomaniac stood in front of the women, who were wearing their formal evening gowns once again, and held a rose in each of his hands.

"Georgia," Balls announced with a smile as the camera cut to the raven-haired beauty beaming before showing the other three women biting their lips.

Georgia glided toward Balls and accepted the first rose while getting a peck on her alabaster cheek.

Then there was a tense, dramatic pause with shots of all three women's faces. Another Oscar for Victoria, Cyr decided in his mind.

"Victoria," Balls finally said with a broad grin.

"Yes! That's our girl!" Bake shouted, high-fiving Cyr, who smiled despite being an emotional wreck on the inside. G52 remained stoic.

Victoria came forward to accept the second rose and a kiss on her cheek while Lucy and Sandy looked crushed -- far more genuinely than Cyr could have expected. *This guy must be some used car salesman in person,* he mused.

"And there you have it," the host said into the camera. "Tomorrow night's live finale is all set. Either Georgia or Victoria will become the king's choice for queen of the United Kingdom of

179

America. Join us at 10 p.m. Eastern Standard Time for the big decision. The king also wants your input. Text your choice with the numbers on the screen and King Robert will take your votes into careful consideration. Thank you for your participation, thank you for watching tonight and we'll see you again tomorrow night right here on the UKA network. Good night."

Chapter 25

Date: March 19, 2036
Place: Aboard the Rendezvous Two in the
western Pacific Ocean

Victoria Kensington rode the glass elevator
down to the first deck of King Ballentine's ship.
Queen finalist or not, she knew she was pressing her
luck. Though no one had told her directly, she was
well aware that none of the women were welcome
to snoop around near the crew cabins and engine
rooms. But Victoria's gut told her it was time to
start getting some answers. President Quigley had to
be held prisoner somewhere in the bowels of the
Rendezvous Two.

When the glass door opened, the pony-tailed
teen -- wearing just an orange bikini -- slowly
padded down the narrow, chessboard-carpeted
corridor. There were closed beige cabin doors on
her right and left. It was louder down here and
Victoria's stomach grew increasingly queasy from
the choppy Pacific's ebb and flow, not to mention
her risky sojourn to this forbidden deck of the ship.

No better time than now. They can't kill off one of the two finalists before the finale or there'll be no friggin' show, she told herself.

Victoria thought she heard voices coming from a cabin door on the left about 20 feet down from the elevator. She leaned her ear against it to listen, but the ambient noise from the engine rooms further down the hall made it tough to hear. *Come on President Quigley, say something quick! Let me know you're in there.* But all she heard was inaudible talking, perhaps a man speaking into a phone.

Then the door diagonally across the corridor on the right suddenly opened and one of Ballentine's huge bodyguards, armed with a holstered pistol, practically walked right into Victoria. She froze, completely busted in eavesdropping position. The blond-haired, hazel-eyed guard -- who wore a black short-sleeved shirt stretched by his bulging biceps, khaki shorts and black-and-gold sneakers -- growled at her.

"What are you doing on this deck?" he asked, grabbing Victoria by both arms with his huge hands and practically shoving his pointy nose in her face. She was so scared she didn't respond right away.

"Answer me girl -- you don't belong down here and you know it," he barked as his unrelenting eyes bore into her from close range.

"I got lost," was all Victoria managed to come up with, knowing full well how feeble that sounded.

"Yeah, that's a very bad lie," the guard said, though he released his grip on her and stepped back a bit to leer at her mostly naked body. "Quite unbecoming of a queen to be caught sneaking around where she ain't supposed to be."

"I'm sorry," Victoria pleaded, weighing whether she should attempt to pummel the guy before he ratted her out to Ballentine. *I beat up Ventana, but this goon might be even bigger ... and he's got a gun.*

"Go back to where you belong and don't let me catch you down on this deck again or I'll cut off your pretty little head and chum the water with it, understood?" the guard warned her in a menacingly sincere voice.

"Completely understood," Victoria replied meekly and nervously, turning and marching back toward the glass elevator in full retreat mode. She could feel his creepy, sinister eyes undressing her ass as she walked and it sent shivers up her spine. She bowed her head and never looked back. She didn't lift her head again until the elevator took her above the first deck, well away from the guard's stare.

Victoria quickly returned to her cabin and locked the door. She grabbed a bottled water from the small fridge and gazed out her window to the sea as she took a drink. The clouds had darkened and the waves had grown bigger on this late Wednesday afternoon.

I'm warmer still, she thought. *The president has to be on the first deck. I'd stake my life on it ... I almost just did. I should be hospitalized for suicidal tendencies. This is crazy ... I just want to go back to high school and be a kid again. Is that too much to ask?*

A knock on her door jarred her from her thoughts.

"Miss Kensington," Howard Nelson's voice said.

"Yes, Howard?" she asked.

"I have good news and an invitation for you if you have a minute to talk," Nelson replied.

The harmless tone in his voice convinced her it was OK to open the door and let him in.

"Again, great job last night. You're getting a ton of votes from the kingdom's viewers," Ballentine's flak told her excitedly as he entered the room and tried not to look too obviously at her gorgeous bikini body. Clearly, he was not aware of her most recent transgression on the first deck. "The king wanted me to let you know that he's invited you to dinner tonight up in the sky lounge on the top deck. There will be a special guest as well so dress nicely."

"OK," Victoria said. "What time?"

"8 p.m.," Nelson said.

"I'll be there," she confirmed with a wink and nod.

"Great, see you at 8," Nelson said, smiling warmly before departing and closing her cabin door.

A special guest? Could it be her ... me? I wouldn't put it past Balls. He must be champing at the bit to get us in the same room ... at the same dinner table ... staring us up and down with those penetrating blue eyes of his. Why do I feel like I'm walking directly into another trap? Probably because I am. That's what I excel at.

"Maybe it's for the best," she told herself out loud. "Something needs to happen fast -- good, bad or ugly. Otherwise I'm going to be this asshole's queen by 3 o'clock tomorrow."

Chapter 26

Date: March 19, 2036
Place: Aboard the Rendezvous Two in the western Pacific Ocean

"The evidence is now overwhelming, Bob -- she needs to go," said Andre Belanger, King Ballentine's most trusted bodyguard. "I just caught her listening outside doors on the first deck. She was within 15 feet of finding the president's cabin."

Ballentine, wearing a black bathrobe and his hair down after a shower, was stretched out on a black leather sofa in the cozy sky lounge den trying to catch a nap before dinner. Dreadlocked Jamaican chef Willie Rhoden was stirring in the kitchen quarters to their left. The lounge's spacious dining room was outside the door Belanger had just entered. The 6-foot-4, 240-pound blond bodyguard stood before the king looking rather annoyed.

"She's a skinny little unarmed bikini-wearing girl and you're one of 10 armed guards I've got patrolling this ship -- do I really have to worry about her? I think I can handle her, mate, if you can't," Balls barked at his security chief as he sat up on the sofa. "I can't just get rid of her now anyway -- she's made the final two."

Belanger shook his head and folded his burly arms across his chest.

"I think you're flirting with disaster, mate," he said with a gruff voice. "Do you even want to hear the results of the fingerprints we took off her wine glass last night or should I just save my breath?"

"Oh, go ahead, tell me so I can piss my pants," Ballentine scoffed, standing up and waving his arms wildly.

"She's an *exact* match with the president," Belanger said with bulging hazel eyes.

"Exact? How is that even possible?" Balls asked.

"I have no idea, mate. They're 52 years apart, but they certainly appear to be carbon copies of one another," Belanger said. "She must be some kind of clone, drone or whatever."

"Then she's here to rescue her twin, is that what you're telling me?" Balls asked with exaggerated hand gestures.

"I sure as hell don't think she's here to fall in love with you," Belanger said, pointing at the king. "In fact, I think there's a very good chance she's here to kill you somehow -- that would be my threat assessment. You already told me you were suspicious of her name -- Victoria Kensington is absurd."

"I thought it was fate at first -- I grew up in Melbourne, which is in Victoria state. Kensington was just down the road, also in Victoria state. Too good to be true, I suppose," Balls said, shaking his head and yawning.

"You're taking this so lightly, Bob -- have you actually fallen for this skinny little girl, as you call her, in just two days?" Belanger asked with crazed eyes.

"I would like to make her my queen, yes, but clearly you're advising against that," Balls said bitterly.

"You would do so at your own peril," the bodyguard said firmly. "She is not who she says she is, so that makes her a liar. She's also a freak of nature -- or the creation of some other enemy force -- because she's an exact clone of your prized hostage, who she's been trying to locate since she arrived on this yacht. Howard told you she asked where Quigley was being kept yesterday. Today she almost found her. Doesn't any of that register on your internal threat assessment meter, Bob?"

"My assessment, Andre, is that she's curious," Balls snapped. "She's an American girl. She knows I have the president. I interviewed the woman on TV. What kid doesn't want to meet the president?"

Belanger shook his head, rolled his eyes up toward the ceiling and started to walk toward the door. Before he departed, he looked back and offered his final warning.

"Don't let that skinny little girl ruin all your grand plans, mate, because I'm telling you right now she's a credible threat," Belanger said. "She's a wild card. You'd be a fool to underestimate her and whoever sent her here."

"Well, it just so happens -- because of my own *curiosity* -- that I'm about to have dinner with our mystery girl and the president in the next room at 8 o'clock," Balls said. "So I'll grill them both and see which one burns."

"I'd be happy to help drill some answers out of the girl, Bob," Belanger added with a devious smile.

"I'm sure you would, Andre," Balls said, lightening up a bit and grinning. "Stay tuned. Depending on what happens, I just might throw you a piece of meat before the night is done."

Chapter 27

Date: March 19, 2036
Place: Aboard the "Rendezvous Two" in the western Pacific Ocean

Victoria Kensington followed Howard Nelson into the elegant sky lounge dining room wearing a flowing black dress and her black hair down over her shoulders. She carried a black-and-gold clutch in her right hand that she had found in one of the dresser drawers and stood nearly 6 feet tall in black heels. With plenty of dark eye shadow and long, black eyelashes, Victoria arrived prepared for a stare-down with her would-be king: black vs. black.

Nelson seated Victoria at a triangular table with one chair to her left, no chair to her right and a spectacular view of the Pacific straight ahead. The carpet was all black in this dimly lit lounge. *No chessboard pattern up here. I'm deep in enemy territory,* Victoria thought as she glanced around warily. A red, three-candle centerpiece adorned the white table cloth as classical music played softly in the large room full of empty tables and chairs. She

190

looked again at the lack of a chair to her right. *This confirms it. The president is definitely coming to dinner and she must still be confined to a wheelchair.*

"The others should be here shortly, Miss Kensington," Nelson said with a cordial smile. He wore a black suit, silver tie and black shoes. "Can I get you some wine?"

"Yes, an Australian red would be perfect, Howard, thank you," Victoria replied with a slight grin.

"Very well," Nelson said before departing and heading through a door at the far end of the dining room.

Moments later, Victoria's heart skipped two beats as the bodyguard who grabbed her on the first deck entered the dining room through the near door. He rolled the wheelchair-bound president toward her table and into the chair-less void to her right. The gray-haired woman with the sad blue eyes, matching blue gown and no jewels or makeup looked straight at her as Victoria froze in her chair. The bodyguard stared at Victoria as well, flashing a creepy, satisfied smile.

"Is this who you were looking for on the first deck, Miss *Kensington*?" the blond giant asked, verbally contorting her alias as if he knew 100 percent that it was bogus.

Victoria tried to collect herself and adapt to the tense, surreal situation. There were two Margeaux Quigleys at the same table and this badass bodyguard seemed hungry for a twin killing.

Where's Ventana and his team now when I really need them? Nowhere to be found, of course.

"Yes, I always wanted to meet the president," Victoria said, tapping into whatever boldness she had left in her drained reserves. "I've been looking forward to this dinner since Howard told me there would be a special guest. I was hoping it would be her and my wish has come true."

"Indeed. Some of my wishes appear to be coming true as well," he sneered while unashamedly undressing her with his eyes again. Victoria quickly looked away and focused on President Quigley, who was studying her in quiet disbelief while she waited for the goon to leave them alone. Mercifully, he did.

"The king will be along shortly," the guard growled before he walked toward the door, blatantly looking back at Victoria with malicious intent, and exited the dining room.

Finally, Victoria was alone with President Quigley. *So this is how I'll look when I get old -- let's see if I can live past tonight first.*

"Who are you?" the president asked, putting on her eyeglasses and leaning toward Victoria for a closer look. "That's bizarre. You look exactly like me when I was a girl. Should I know you? What are you doing here?"

Victoria sipped her wine and smiled even though she was mostly at a loss for words. *This is the woman I've been trying to find. Now I have no idea what to say, where to begin?*

"I am in the contest to be King Ballentine's queen and I've made the finals," she said, figuring

192

she was very likely being watched on a hidden camera as she spoke. "Have you seen the show, Madam President?"

Quigley scowled at the notion. "Certainly not," she said. "I wouldn't watch that egomaniac murderer and his rubbish. I only appeared in a TV interview with him because they literally stuck a gun to my head. You are from America, correct?"

"Yes, I'm Victoria Kensington from Newport, Rhode Island," she said, smiling as she recalled a slogan Cyr had shared with her that the state used in the 1980s to advertise itself to potential tourists. "Rhode Island is the biggest little state in the union."

"Hah, union," Quigley scoffed. "What union? I've been forgotten out here in the middle of nowhere with no hope of rescue while the *union* has crumbled without a fight. Your so-called king has been allowed to rule in absentia from the high seas and frolic with foolish, treasonous tarts like yourself. You're young enough to be his granddaughter, for crying out loud! Don't you have any self-respect?" the president said, pounding the table with her right fist.

"Not enough, apparently. How's your leg?" Victoria asked, desperate to change the subject and tenor of the conversation.

"Better than I'm letting on," the president said fearlessly while clutching her wheelchair with both hands.

"Um, they're probably watching us right now," Victoria said with alarmed eyes and a hushed tone.

"Of course they are," the president replied, pointing up toward a tinted black ball anchored within a brass chandelier about 12 feet away to the left. "I don't care. What else can they do to me? They've already killed my husband, shot me, kidnapped me and hijacked my entire country. Back in the day, thieves liked to pull off car-jackings. Today they've upped their game. They prefer country-jackings. What a wonderful world it has turned out to be."

Victoria felt flustered as the president rambled through her harangue. *I better just let her vent. She certainly has plenty to bitch about. But so do I. If she only knew what hell I've gone through to get here, and what hell is still to come if I don't figure out something fast. I have to find a way to slip her the $100 bill I wrote my message to her on without them getting even more suspicious of me. There's got to be a way. Think. Think!*

"Madam President, may I please have your autograph?" Victoria asked, pulling a silver pen and the $100 bill out of her clutch. She laid them flat on the table in front of Quigley.

"My autograph? What's the point of that, you silly girl?" the president huffed, but she also watched as Victoria's red-polished finger nail pointed to some small words written in black ink on the white periphery of the bill. Quigley leaned forward, read quickly and toned down her rant as the words sank in: *"Your stepson Bill sent me in an attempt to track me and find you -- what cabin are they keeping you in? Tell me a number as part of regular conversation. Bill loves you and misses you. I will find a way to rescue you."*

The president eyed Victoria in a whole different way, paused to think for a second and turned the bill over to sign it.

"There you go young lady -- my autograph -- for all its worth these days, probably 17 cents," Quigley said smoothly.

Victoria nodded at the number while the president raised her eyes to alert her new ally to the enemy closing in from the door at the rear of the dining room. The teen quickly slid the pen back into the clutch, turned her body to the right to use her back as a shield, crumpled the $100 bill into a small wad, popped it into her mouth and swallowed it whole. Fortunately for her, King Ballentine's eyes were fixed on and delighted by the president's scowl at that moment.

Ballentine -- dressed all in black as usual with a crimson tie and platinum Rolex watch but no crown -- strolled to the table alongside a young male server.

"Your Australian red, Miss Kensington -- a clever suggestion," Balls said, looking down at her with a smug smirk as the server poured the wine into Victoria's glass and then into Ballentine's glass. "Just water as usual for the former president, Ralph."

"Thank you and good evening, King Ballentine," Victoria said, not sure whether to stand up or kiss his hand. She did neither. *Who's wooing who here? I'm not sucking up to this creep anymore.* Fortunately, he sat down to her left as the server filled all of their water glasses and then departed.

"Thank you, Ralph, and good evening, ladies," Balls said, now displaying an almost-giddy smile as he leaned closer to them. "You both look fabulous tonight."

"Thank you," Victoria replied.

"Flattery will go nowhere with me -- I don't know about this one," the president said bitterly as she nodded toward Victoria.

The king remained visibly amused as he spent several seconds staring at each of them and comparing their faces in his twisted mind.

"Chef Willie has prepared some grilled steak and coconut shrimp with garlic mashed potatoes and fresh spring asparagus for us this evening -- how does that sound, ladies? Any special requests?" Ballentine asked.

"My unconditional release," the president said flatly, staring right at him.

Victoria had to smile at her willful spirit. The king also grinned and took a gulp of red wine.

"Into the Pacific?" he quipped. "What a waste of such a prized catch."

When Ralph returned with a basket of rolls and three cups of lobster bisque to get the meal started, Victoria decided to send up a verbal weather balloon.

"So king, what are my chances against Georgia in the finale tomorrow?" she asked before sampling the bisque with her spoon.

"I'm so glad you asked, Miss Kensington. I'd say anywhere from zero to zero," Ballentine said, closely gauging her reaction.

Victoria hesitated, the spoon practically lodging in her mouth for a second, but then she tried to act cool as she swallowed the hot bisque. She looked straight ahead toward the Pacific. *Now I really wish I had thrown him overboard yesterday when I had the chance.* Balls thoroughly enjoyed watching her flinch and mull her next move.

"Why zero? Does Georgia really do it for you?" Victoria asked with an edge to her voice Ballentine had never heard before.

The president abruptly stopped eating and clanged her spoon against the cup.

"Excuse me, but do I really need to be here? I don't want to be the third wheel for this idiotic dog-and-pony show," she interrupted as Ballentine and Victoria glared at each other. "The two of you can sort out your dirty laundry yourselves and leave me out of it."

"No, former president, I really think you should stick around to hear this," Balls said, putting his hand on Quigley's shoulder, causing her to recoil in disgust. "Not to mention, Ralph has returned to bring us our splendid main course."

The tall, lanky server dressed all in black knifed through the tension at the triangular table for a moment as he delivered three hot plates of sizzling rib-eye steak, jumbo coconut shrimp, garlic mashed potatoes and asparagus as promised. Ballentine waited for Ralph to exit before he

197

directed his attention back to Victoria. He wasn't smiling anymore.

"At least Georgia is a real person," the king said loudly, leaning toward Victoria with an angry face.

Stay calm, stay cool. Black, black, black -- be powerful, too, Victoria thought.

"And I'm not real as I sit here before you?" she countered sharply, her blue-and-black eyes boldly challenging him through flickering candlelight.

Ballentine didn't reply. He looked down at his plate, slowly carved into his steak, took a big bite and then glared at her. He chewed for what seemed like an eternity while never taking his icy blue eyes off hers. Nervous as she was on the inside, Victoria stared right back, defiant as ever. The soothing sound of violins overhead did nothing to soften the harsh silence between them.

The president watched the confrontation with more interest now. She was impressed with the teenager's strength, resolve and poise against such an imposing person. *This girl is me,* Quigley thought. *How is this possible? I must be dreaming. And how the hell is she going to rescue me?*

Ballentine interrupted the president's thoughts when he finally broke the silent showdown with Victoria.

"I'm only going to say this one time and I want an honest answer. Who are you?" he asked the girl.

"I'm Victoria …," she started to lie.

"No, you're not!" Balls shouted, pounding his right fist on the table with the fork still in his hand and the big steak knife in his left hand.

"Kensington, Victoria, is a place just down the road from where I grew up in Melbourne. You are a figment of someone's imagination. Your fingerprints, which we lifted off your wine glass in the waterfall lounge last night, match the woman sitting to your right *exactly*. You've been trying to find the woman sitting to your right since you set foot on this ship. Well, mystery girl, here she is. We've called your bluff. Who are you and what do you want to do with the president? Or would you prefer to take your steak knife and stab me through the heart with it right now?"

Victoria sat stunned throughout Ballentine's diatribe, but she didn't flinch this time. She refused to give him the satisfaction. The president, meanwhile, put her overburdened head in her hands. *Is this what passes for a rescue mission these days -- send a teenager with a horrible alias? My stepson has sealed this poor girl's fate and mine,* she lamented.

Victoria took a sip of red wine and gathered her strength for a moment.

"Go fuck yourself asshole!" she finally erupted. "You're only a king in your own fucked-up mind!"

"That's all you have to say -- no explanation, no more lies?" Balls asked with a crazed look.

"No, I was speaking the truth just then. There's plenty more that I could say, but I won't," Victoria seethed.

Andre Belanger and another armed guard were approaching the dining room. Victoria sensed their presence before they even burst through the door. *Let them win this battle,* she ordered herself. *There will be another chance. Tomorrow. During the finale show. Clearly, I won't be in the show. Just stay alive until then -- somehow.*

Ballentine sneered at Victoria as his guards now stood behind her chair.

"She just told me to go fuck myself, can you believe that, Andre?" Balls told his security chief with a snort. Belanger and his cohort laughed loudly behind her.

Then Balls leaned his wretched face so close to hers he almost touched her left cheek with his nose. His breath reeked.

"I could say the same to you, little girl, and you actually could go fuck yourself -- you and the president are one in the same, you lying punk!" he shouted, showering spittle onto her nose, lips and cheeks. Victoria froze in horror. Belanger and his cohort laughed again. Quigley closed her eyes and said a prayer.

Ballentine got up from the table and stepped back as the guards seized Victoria by the arms and stood her up. She left her clutch on her chair.

"This dinner is over and so are you," the king commanded with a booming voice as he scowled at her. "Mystery girl, you have been disqualified from the queen contest for lying about your identity and posing as a threat to myself and the new United Kingdom of America. Lucy Sanchez will replace you in tomorrow's finale. Andre and Walter will escort you to your new cabin on the first deck. I've heard you love to snoop around down there so now you get to rot down there. They will interrogate you all night tonight and all day tomorrow if they have to. If you provide them with truthful answers about yourself, who created you and who sent you, they may spare you some unpleasantries and, possibly, but not likely, spare your life. Are we clear?"

Her alias exposed but her courage still intact, young Margeaux Quigley stood tall in her black heels and kept her eyes fixed squarely on Ballentine's angry face.

"We'll see who *spears* who," she said, burning with hatred for the black king.

Chapter 28

Date: March 19, 2036
Place: Aboard the Rendezvous Two in the western Pacific Ocean

Andre and Walter led young Margeaux Quigley to a cabin on the first deck that was very similar to the one she stayed in on the second deck, yet it seemed much smaller. Perhaps that was because two large goons were occupying this room with her.

"Walter and I will be your babysitters for the time being," Andre growled as he paced behind her chair, sending shivers up Margeaux's spine as she faced the Pacific. Walter partially blocked her ocean view as he leaned against the window ledge. He was shorter, but stocky and formidable in his own way. He had short, curly black hair with black stubble all over his face and neck. He wore a navy blue hooded sweatshirt, blue jeans and black sneakers. His breath smelled of onions and cigarettes. But Margeaux was more concerned about the black pistol he was aiming at her chest.

"Take off the evening dress, girl, and everything else while you're at it," Walter said with a menacing voice and cold, charcoal eyes.

Andre smiled and returned to stand next to Walter for a full frontal view of what was to come. His pistol was sticking out of the waistband of his black gym shorts. He also wore a black muscle shirt and black-and-gold sneakers.

"Will that really be necessary?" Margeaux protested.

"We find that naked prisoners feel more vulnerable and prove more helpful answering our questions," Andre replied with a condescending tone.

"Do I have your word that you will respect my wish not to be fucked by either of you or any of your other cronies?" Margeaux asked with all the willfulness she could muster as her head ached and her hopes vanished.

Andre and Walter both chuckled. "No, you definitely don't have our word on that," Walter said with a wide, lustful grin.

"See, at least we gave you an honest answer," Andre sneered. "So far, you've proven to be nothing but a liar -- except about your virginity. I'll give you credit for that. And Walter and I both appreciate that you've saved yourself for us."

"Yes, personally I'm very touched," Walter quipped.

"So the truth is we both plan on fucking you sooner or later, but we'd also like to get some information out of you," Andre said with hungry hazel eyes. "The first thing we'd like you to do is strip. Do it or we'll be happy to help you do it."

Margeaux scowled at both of them, but she slowly obeyed, stripping down to her bare skin and dumping her clothes on the chessboard carpet. She put her left forearm across her breasts and her right hand over her thin black landing strip. That attempt to conceal herself didn't last long. Walter took her arms behind her back and handcuffed her to the back of the chair. Now the guards could lean back against the window ledge and admire the view of their naked 17-year-old prisoner. Choppy waves rocked the large ship, making Margeaux feel queasy as she looked down to avoid Andre and Walter's lustful stares. They both pictured themselves fucking her and remained silent for several creepy moments. *Death would be a welcome alternative to this,* Margeaux thought to herself as tears welled up in her eyes.

Then came the probing questions.

"Who are you really and who sent you here?" Walter asked her, bending down to look her in the eyes and get a better view of her mouthful-sized, pouty breasts.

Margeaux suddenly looked up and met his disgusting gaze.

"Who cares?" she replied, not blinking.

"I do," Walter said angrily. "Answer the fucking question."

"No," she said.

Walter slapped her across the face with his left hand as he held the pistol in his right hand. Then his left hand squeezed her right breast hard enough to make her cry out in pain. Margeaux's left cheek reddened and stung badly from the slap. She winced and began to twitch in the chair. She could feel a seizure coming on. What little control she had left would soon be gone. *I'm done for,* she feared.

Then she heard the monotone voice of G52 reverberate through her brain. "You hold all of the cards in the deck -- use them," the alien said. *He told me that when I was eating lunch with Jimmy Baker. How stupid that sounds now,* she lamented. *I hate you all for putting me in this position.*

The seizure took hold of her, but the alien's voice persisted in her mind, nagging her to "use all of her cards" again and again.

Margeaux's naked body convulsed in the chair. Her eyes began rolling back and she foamed at the mouth. Walter recoiled from her and stood up. He and Andre both looked confused.

"What the fuck is wrong with her?" Walter asked.

"I have no clue," Andre replied distractedly. He became aroused watching the handcuffed girl's nubile breasts and thighs jerk from side to side in the chair. "But it sure doesn't look like she's faking it."

"Shouldn't we just throw her on the bed and fuck the shit out of her?" Walter suggested with a hopeful voice. "That might cure her."

"No, Balls told me to try to get some answers out of her before we fucked her, otherwise she'll have no reason to give us anything," Andre said.

"Then you shouldn't have told her we were planning to fuck her sooner or later," Walter said.

"Good point," Andre said. "That's what happens when you start thinking with the wrong head, mate. Worst-case scenario, even if she doesn't tell us anything, I'm fucking her tomorrow while Balls is filming his show and you get sloppy seconds right after me."

"What a deal," Walter said sarcastically.

"It's better than sloppy tenths," Andre pointed out. "Would you prefer that? Would you prefer to go after anal Artie, dip-shit Dennis, VD Victor and all the rest?"

"Hell no," Walter said, his eyes refocusing on the teen's violent seizure. "Seconds will be just fine, mate."

"I thought so," Andre said, still leering at Margeaux despite her unattended medical situation.

A sudden knock on the door snapped them out of their sex-crazed daze.

"Who the fuck is that?" Walter wondered, raising his pistol warily.

"Well go find out," Andre ordered him.

Walter scurried to the door and leaned against it. "Who is it?" he asked with an angry voice. But there was only an eerie silence after that one strange, hard knock. Walter pointed his pistol with his right hand and opened the door in a swift motion with his left hand.

"No one," he said before glancing down at the chessboard-carpeted hallway floor. "Andre, look at this."

The blond giant joined him at the cabin door's entrance. There were playing cards scattered outside the door and all the way up the hallway toward the glass elevator. Some cards were face-up, others were face-down with solid black backings. They were the same cards Balls played with on the gaming tables in the waterfall lounge.

"Who the hell is playing games?" Walter shouted down the empty corridor as the ship rocked violently in high seas. There was no answer.

"Look at the cards, mate," Andre told him, stooping down to inspect them. He also began turning over the cards that were face down. "Diamonds, hearts, clubs and spades, but they're all queens, Walter."

Walter's black eyes bugged out. "Talk about a stacked deck," he said.

"Yeah, and I'm beginning to think we're fucking with the wrong card in the deck, mate," Andre said ominously.

Chapter 29

Date: March 20, 2036
Place: Aboard the Rendezvous Two in the western Pacific Ocean

There were no more knocks on the door in the overnight hours other than from Andre and Walter. Ballentine's guards took turns keeping watch over their 17-year-old naked prisoner every two hours while sleeping in their own cabins in between.

Young Margeaux was weak, listless and disoriented after her seizure. Andre let her sleep nude on the bed, but kept her handcuffed just in case. The inexplicable deck of queens scattered out in the hallway had sufficiently freaked out both him and Walter. Seizure or not, they refused to underestimate the girl.

When Margeaux finally woke up at 8:30 a.m. on Thursday, the day of the queen contest live finale show, Andre was sitting in the chair across from the bed. His arms were folded across his chest, his pistol was still protruding from the waistband of his black shorts, and a weird, almost befuddled expression had taken over his normally sinister, self-assured face.

"What did you do to me? What happened?" Margeaux asked, slowly sitting up on the bed before looking embarrassed and horrified as she realized she was still naked. The only positive change was she felt recharged from an extremely deep sleep.

"Nothing happened," Andre said, leaning toward her with a scowl on his face and pulling out the deck of cards he had picked up out in the corridor. "You answered none of our questions, you had a seizure, we didn't fuck you yet and here we are. But we did find this deck of cards tossed out in the hallway -- 52 queens as a matter of fact. You wouldn't know anything about that, would you? Are you a magician, voodoo virgin or something? Do you enjoy performing card tricks?"

Margeaux rubbed the sleep out of her eyes with her handcuffed hands and then quickly put them back in front of her private area. "I remember I started to have a seizure after your asshole buddy slapped my face and squeezed my breast. That's about it," she said bitterly. "So don't accuse me of anything. I've been your handcuffed prisoner, under your complete control and at your mercy the whole time. You've treated me like a piece of shit."

Andre smiled lustily. "Oh, we're just getting warmed up, darling," he sneered. "You better start talking -- there's a countdown clock on you losing your virginity many times over. You've got less than six hours to go."

Margeaux shuddered at the thought and felt sick to her stomach, but she took some comfort in that she had survived the night and that she had a very similar countdown clock ticking for the guards and Ballentine. She knew she had to summon all the strength she had -- as well as all the strength she didn't know she had -- for the 2 o'clock hour.

"You do what you have to and so will I," the teenager snapped right back at Andre.

"What is that supposed to mean?" he growled, putting a hand on his pistol.

A knock on the door interrupted them.

"It's Walter," Andre's cohort said before entering a second later and closing the door behind him.

"You're early, what's going on?" Andre asked.

Walter's scruffy face looked puzzled. "Artie on the second deck told me some crazy shit about last night, mate," he said before distracting himself with an eyeful of Margeaux.

"Not in front of her," Andre said, quickly springing off the chair, opening the door and ushering Walter back into the hall. "What happened -- something to do with the deck of cards?

"Maybe," Walter said in a hushed tone as Andre left the door open only a crack behind him.

Margeaux scooted to the edge of the bed, but she could only hear whispers. She was just as curious to find out what that abusive prick Walter had to say.

"Artie told me he was patrolling down the end of the second deck corridor and he swears he looked back and saw a naked girl walk out of the glass elevator. She walked right into the room where this one used to stay," Walter said, nodding toward

Margeaux, "and where the president is now being held."

"What the fuck, mate? She's been here the whole fucking time -- I'd swear my life on it," Andre whispered as he flailed his huge right arm in the air.

"It gets even stranger," Walter said. "Artie followed the girl into the president's room, but it was just the president sleeping in the bed. No sign of anyone. Then he ducked back into the hallway and the naked girl was getting back onto the elevator. He said the girl just stared at him. He yelled at her and chased after her, but she disappeared down the elevator. He rode it down a minute later but never saw her again."

Andre shook his head. "This one swears she knows nothing about the cards," he said, nodding toward the room.

"I told Artie about the cards we found down here, mate, and it freaked him out even more," Walter said. "Should we tell Balls about all this crazy shit?"

"No," Andre said without hesitation. "We'll fuck the truth out of this girl later today and then we'll tell ghost stories tonight over a few beers. Balls will have his new queen by then and we could all use a good laugh. If I get my way, we'll push this voodoo girl overboard while we're at it and let the sharks finish her off."

"The sooner, the better," Walter whispered with a haunted look.

Chapter 30

Date: March 20, 2036
Place: Area 52, Kingsbury, Nevada
Bill Cyr, Jimmy Baker and the alien G52 were
back in the L-shaped room to view the queen finale
show on the UKA network. It was 7 p.m. Nevada
time, 10 p.m. on the East Coast.

The bad news hit Cyr like a sucker punch to the
stomach.

"Victoria Kensington has been disqualified in
the past 24 hours because she lied about her
identity," host Howard Nelson informed viewers at
the beginning of the show. "However, Lucy
Sanchez has been brought back to compete with
Georgia Fulmer to be King Robert Ballentine's
queen of the United Kingdom of America. The king
has taken your texted votes for Georgia into
consideration, but Lucy will be given another
chance to win over the king in tonight's live finale."

Cyr turned off the TV and flung the bowl of
popcorn across the room, much like young

Margeaux had done just a few days ago. Bake looked alarmed but, for a change, didn't say a word. He had never seen Cyr get upset before. He felt bad about Margeaux, too. She was his classmate in Spanish after all, but clearly, something had gone horribly wrong.

G52 attempted to change the mood, rolling toward the wall of TVs so he could get their full attention. His two rear digital-green eyes now faced them even though the front of him pointed toward the blank screens.

"I have sent the young woman messages telepathically instructing her to use all of her super effects," the alien said in his usual monotone.

"How will we know if your messages got through, 52?" Cyr asked dejectedly. "They might've killed her already. I never should've sent her -- it just shows how low and desperate we've become."

"Do not underestimate what this young woman can do," 52 persisted. "If cornered, she will likely be at her strongest and most lethal."

"She's still just one girl," Cyr said.

"One girl to the 52nd power," the alien corrected him. "And the queen is the most powerful piece."

"Well it sounds like she won't be queen -- she's been disqualified, 52," Cyr pointed out.

"Black king may say she's not a queen and treat her like a pawn, but she has been promoted whether he likes it or not," 52 said. "I predict black king will soon be the piece that is cornered."

Cyr shook his head and rubbed his weary eyes.

"You see everything in black and white, 52, but there are a lot of variables, a lot of gray areas in this situation," Cyr said. "We still have no clue where she is, how many armed thugs are guarding her or how many Chinese ships are surrounding the boat she's on. The harsh reality is we may never see Margeaux Quigley-17 again and we may never find the president."

"False. I would still bet on white to win this match," 52 countered.

"For the sake of everyone in the free world, I hope you're right, 52," Cyr said.

Chapter 31

Date: March 20, 2036

Place: Aboard the Rendezvous Two in the western Pacific Ocean

Young Margeaux was still naked and handcuffed on the bed at 2 p.m. She refused any offers of food and was forced to use the toilet in front of Andre and Walter. She had not uttered a word during the guards' three additional attempts to pump her for information. Now they were eager to hump her -- information or not.

"You get started and I'll take some video as a memento because we're gonna miss her when we dump her bare ass overboard," Walter said to Andre as he stood near the bed with his smart phone camera ready.

"That's right, it's party time, mate," Andre said, quickly removing his black muscle shirt, gym shorts, gun, underwear and sneakers. He dumped them on the chair and jumped onto the bed. The smart phone he had stashed in his shorts fell out of a pocket and onto the carpet with a soft thud. A text message light was flashing, but both guards failed to notice. Their minds were focused on one thing -- sex.

Rape. I can't believe I'm about to be raped by two Neanderthals, Margeaux thought, as she closed her eyes and remained rigid, sitting in an upright position on the bed with her handcuffed hands over her breasts. Andre easily pushed her backward onto the tropical-themed sheets until her head fell on the pillow. He loomed over her with massive biceps, shoulders and chest, ravenous hazel eyes and a hard cock ready to poke her. His mouth was open and stinking of beer. When the blond giant attempted to enter her, she wriggled her lower body left and right to avoid his member.

"Stop doing this to me!" she screamed. "I don't deserve this!"

"Oh, so now you know how to talk, little girl. Isn't that funny. Just shut up and take it," Andre said, grabbing her slim hips with his powerful hands as she struggled.

Walter smiled and enjoyed being the voyeur with the small camera capturing it all. He also pictured himself mounting the sexy teenager next. *Not your average afternoon on the high seas today,* he mused, as saliva flooded his hungry tongue.

One single hard knock on the door made Walter jump and Andre freeze.

"Now what?" Andre shouted.

"Who is it?" Walter yelled at the door. "Go away!"

"It's me," a woman's voice shouted back. "I want to join the fun in there."

216

"What?" Andre asked in disbelief as he sat on the bed with his cock up and his eyes darting from the door to his gun on the chair and back again. "Go see who it is, Walter. Shoot first and ask questions later."

Walter warily crept to the door, putting his camera phone in the left front pocket of his blue jeans, grabbing the pistol out of his holster belt with his right hand and turning the door knob slowly with his left hand. He opened the door a crack and peered into the corridor. He couldn't believe his eyes. It was another completely naked teenage girl who looked exactly like their prisoner.

"Don't you want to double your fun?" the girl asked playfully. "I'll pair up with you while they're doing their thing."

Walter leered at her up and down, paralyzed by her beauty.

"Who are you?" he finally asked.

"Really? I'm so tired of being asked that," the girl replied, not so playfully this time. Then she kicked the door open with superhuman force, leveled Walter in the process, grabbed his gun off the floor and aimed it at Andre's cock a split-second before he could reach the chair. He froze, facing the armed-and-dangerous girl like an obscene naked sculpture.

"Touch your gun and I'll blow that one away!" the naked girl shouted, nodding toward his erect penis and kicking the door closed behind her at the same time. "This is a private party. We don't want any other guests right now."

Young Margeaux sat up on the bed and couldn't believe her eyes. *She looks just like me. Stark naked, too.*

Walter moaned, writhing around on the carpet in agony and grabbing his bleeding head. He seemed concussed and completely useless.

"Move your raping ass back toward the window ledge and stay there or I will shoot you full of holes!" the naked girl commanded Andre.

The guard silently obeyed. He slowly raised his hands in a defensive posture as his cock started going in the opposite direction. His desperate eyes stole a few glances at his pistol on the chair.

"So close and yet so far, *mate*," the girl taunted him. "You *almost* reached your gun. You *almost* noticed the text message on your phone warning you about us and what we're capable of. You're way off your game, *mate*. That's because you and this girl-slapping, titty-twisting scumbag here were too busy *almost* raping a virgin. Oops. I *almost* forgot to tell you. Your phone is about to ring."

Sure enough, the ring tone on Andre's phone went off. It was the catchy, familiar melody from "The Pink Panther." The naked girl knelt down, picked up the phone off the floor with her left hand and flipped it to Andre while still aiming Walter's gun at him with her right hand. Andre caught the phone just to the left of his limp dick.

"Answer it," she ordered, moving a couple of steps closer to Andre with her eyes full of venom and her finger itchy on the trigger.

Andre reluctantly punched a button with his thumb and the familiar, bearded face of fellow guard VD Victor appeared on the screen. "Where are you guys? Where is everybody? What the fuck is going on? I just watched Dennis get tossed overboard from the sky deck. He's gone man. Deader than dead."

"Who did it?" Andre asked, his skin turning more pale by the second and his fretful tone suggesting he was gravely afraid of the answer.

"You're not going to believe me if I tell you, mate," Victor said.

"Try me ... I just might," the blond giant replied haltingly.

"I was 40 feet away, but I swear I saw a naked girl send him right over the railing like he was a rag doll," Victor said. "I couldn't believe my ... shit! Stop! No!"

"What? Vic?" Andre asked.

Andre watched his smart phone in horror as Victor got forced backward and hurled overboard, too. The phone's camera quickly lost sight of him, spiraling through the air with rapidly changing views of the white clouds and the blue Pacific. Seconds later, the phone went dead as it pelted the waves.

"And then there were three -- you two pervs and the one guarding the TV show that's going on right now," the naked girl said, glaring at Andre as if he were next and time was running short. "Well, make that four. We don't want to forget the black king. He's the reason we're here after all."

"I don't know who or what you are, but I'm very impressed. Please don't kill me," Andre pleaded with terrified hazel eyes. Now he was the prey, not the predator, and naked at that. "I'll help you kill Balls. I'll pay you lots of money. I'll do anything you want."

"Apparently, we're doing just fine without your help," the naked girl replied. "I only have one question for you."

"What is it?" Andre begged.

"Do you have any idea where we are in the world right now?" she asked.

"Yes, yes I do," Andre slobbered like a dog. "We're about 125 miles southwest of Wake Island, which is a U.S. territory."

"Thanks, you've been a splendid compass," the naked girl said with a killer smile. "My only regret is your plunge will be much shorter than the others. We'll just make sure it's messier, that's all. Now go feed the sharks!"

The naked girl dropped the pistol, charged toward the window with blinding speed and kicked Andre through the thick glass with a force equivalent to 52 extremely pissed-off women. The guard crashed overboard amid shards of glass and plummeted into the ocean. He was swallowed up by the waves and quickly left behind by the fast-moving ship.

Margeaux's jaw dropped open as she watched the whole scene unfold before her eyes. *I do have a team! I'm my own army ... navy ... whatever. This must've been what G52 meant by using all of the cards in my deck.*

Then she watched the naked girl drag groggy Walter by his hoodie across the carpet. "Say hi to Jaws for me, loser!" she shouted bitterly as she flung him out the broken window like a bag of garbage.

"Thank you so much for rescuing me," Margeaux said as the girl quickly fished the keys out of Andre's shorts on the chair and unlocked her handcuffs. "Free at last!"

"There's no time to talk," her heroic doppelganger said, putting a finger to Margeaux's lips. "We have one more guard to deal with and a very important date with the king in the waterfall lounge right now."

"Can I at least put on some clothes?" Margeaux asked.

"No," the girl replied. "There's nothing more powerful than the naked truth of how they treated us. Only the president will be dressed."

"The president?" Margeaux wondered aloud, standing up with a confused look on her face.

"You'll see," the girl said, placing both of her warm hands on Margeaux's bare shoulders in an attempt to reassure her. "The commander-in-chief is now armed and ready to roll, so let's all go crash the king's party upstairs."

Chapter 32

Date: March 20, 2036

Place: Aboard the Rendezvous Two in the western Pacific Ocean

King Balls was having a ball playing Texas Hold 'em poker on live TV with his queen finalists Georgia Fulmer and Lucy Sanchez under the glare of overhead lights.

Jamaican chef Willie Rhoden, wearing a tuxedo and his flowing dreadlocks, doubled as a card dealer for the finale. He flashed his pearly white teeth and smiled at Ballentine while dealing two cards face-down to each player. Balls also wore a tuxedo for the occasion as he sat at the end of a curved casino table facing the length of the vast waterfall lounge. Georgia, with her raven-haired curls cascading down her back, sat to the king's left in a glittering emerald evening gown with a high slit up her right leg and matching heels. To the left of Georgia, Lucy turned up the heat in a leopard-skin mini skirt that hugged all of her curves tightly and long, black heels. They were all drinking Captain Morgan rum and cokes on the rocks with limes, fondling their casino chips and flirting. It was 2:36 p.m. (10:36 p.m. East Coast UKA time) and Ballentine's big decision was scheduled to be made at 2:58 (10:58).

One cameraman was shooting Balls and his would-be queens from behind the bar. Another was kneeling and moving around the casino table for tight shots of Willie, as well as the cards being dealt and held by each player. Two bright, hot lights and a fixed boom mic hovered over the table. Howard Nelson, the show host, watched the card game from his plush black chair on the near end of the hardwood dance floor. He sat under the glare of a light stand, and another man stood next to him with a camera and portable boom mic nearby. An armed guard stood at the far end of the dance floor in between the two exit doors that led to the outdoor swimming pool. All of the heavy black drapes were drawn over the huge windows to give the impression that they were filming at night in a casino lounge, not in the middle of a sunny, sultry afternoon on the high seas. The waves were calm again, and the Rendezvous Two arrowed to the southwest swiftly and smoothly.

During the course of the poker hand, Ballentine noticed his guard Alex -- a 6-foot-2, 220-pound man with a buzz cut, black jumpsuit and black boots -- repeatedly attempt to call someone with his smart phone. He was becoming increasingly agitated that he was apparently not getting through.

"Lucy folded and Georgia raised, King Ballentine. What do you want to do?" Willie asked, trying to regain his attention.

Balls forgot about the guard for the moment and refocused on the two cards in his hand -- the king of clubs and the six of spades. He glanced at the four cards lying face-up on the table -- the four of hearts, the jack of spades, the nine of clubs and the seven of diamonds -- no help there.

"Oh, what the hell," he said, flipping a few chips into the pot to match Georgia. "She's bluffing. She doesn't have anything. I call," he added with a chuckle and a playful left shoulder bump against Georgia's toned, bare right arm.

"We'll see about that," she said confidently before they both revealed their hidden cards.

"Yes! I'm holding pocket queens!" Georgia exulted in her sexy North Carolina drawl as she pumped her left fist. Sure enough, she laid down a queen of diamonds and a queen of hearts with her right hand.

Balls shook his head. "How about that. The best I've got is my lonely old king so far, how fitting," he said with a sheepish grin.

"Good hand, Miss Georgia," Willie said with a smile.

"Hey, it's not over yet, mate," Balls protested. "I've had my share of luck on the river over the years. Show me another king, Chez Willie, and we'll split the loot."

As Willie beamed and prepared to place the deciding "river" card on the green felt table in front of them, Ballentine noticed his guard walk to the door at the far right end of the dance floor. Alex moved the black curtain covering the glass top-half of the door just enough to peer outside without letting much light into the lounge. He paused motionless for a second and then quietly exited through the door.

"You win king!" Willie declared with a big grin as he placed the king of spades down on the table. "A pair of kings beats a pair of queens. Sorry, Miss Georgia."

"Shit!" Georgia said, snapping her fingers in defeat as Balls howled in laughter.

"Ah ha! I warned you that I'm deadly on the river!" he bellowed, heartily quaffing his drink. He pulled most of his newly won chips toward him with one hand while flipping smiling Willie a couple of chips with the other. "I pick up a king on the river and beat pocket queens with a pair of black kings. Sometimes life is a ball."

Then a naked teenage girl slipped into the room through the same door the guard had exited. *She looks an awful lot like Victoria Kensington,* Balls thought, as his heart skipped a beat and his boisterous laughter stopped short. The lounge went silent as all eyes and camera lenses turned toward the young woman who had snared the king's attention. She padded slowly on bare feet across the dimly lit far reaches of the dance floor and gazed directly at Ballentine. Then she raised her right hand to reveal she had a pistol and pointed it toward the casino table. A collective groan could be heard.

"Keep all cameras rolling and someone get that boom mic near me so I can be heard on live TV," the girl ordered. "No one *else* should move and no one *else* will be harmed if these requests are met."

Balls sure didn't like the sound of the word "else." He began to twitch and sweat in his tuxedo as he recalled how Andre Belanger had warned him that this skinny little girl was a threat. The young man next to Howard Nelson grabbed the portable boom mic and strode alongside the naked girl with a stunned look on his face. Nelson gripped his chair with a pair of white-knuckled hands as his eyes bugged out.

"What the hell are you doing here?" Balls asked angrily but remained seated at the table. Lucy and Georgia shivered next to him in shock. Willie froze, too. "This is a live TV show we're filming here."

"I'm well aware of that," young Margeaux Quigley said authoritatively as she approached the table and stepped into the glaring lights with Walter's long lost black pistol pointed at the king's chest. "I hope full nudity is allowed on the UKA network. I wanted to show how I was interrogated by this so-called king's bodyguards on the first deck of the yacht were on. It's called the Rendezvous Two, by the way, and we're about 125 miles or so southwest of Wake Island in the Pacific Ocean. It's actually the middle of the afternoon here, eight hours behind East Coast USA time. I hope you don't mind full disclosure to your live audience, King Balls, as you like to call yourself."

"Where are my guards?" Balls screamed. "Howard, call them at once! Call the Chinese, too!"

"No, Howard, that really won't be necessary. Stay seated right where you are," Margeaux ordered.

The fearful flak remained frozen and bug-eyed.

"I've fed all 10 of your bodyguards to the sharks, just as some of them threatened to do to me on multiple occasions," Margeaux said, still pointing the gun at Balls' chest.

She then eyed his winning hand of two black kings and smiled.

"And I see that you're quite a poker player," she noted with a patronizing tone. "Two kings beat two queens, do they?"

Balls' lips quivered without a response. Naked Margeaux commanded the room and dominated the cameras. Her determined blue eyes bore a hole through her black-and-white prey. The king's sweat made him smell like a skunk, too, something the cameras couldn't capture. But Georgia and Lucy clearly were beginning to struggle with the foul scent.

"I suppose it depends on which game we're playing, doesn't it?" Margeaux said with a smirk as she touched the face-up cards with her left index finger. "See, you might be playing poker, where the king is more powerful than the queen. But all along I've been playing chess, where the queen is the far more powerful piece -- able to travel in many directions at variable speeds; able to trap the king while he's enjoying himself and not paying attention to the game surrounding the game. Yes, all of your protective pawns have been removed -- overboard, off the board, whatever you prefer to call it -- and now it's just you and me, King Balls. You're in check, *mate*."

"What do you want? I'm extremely rich as you can see -- name it and it's yours!" the pony-tailed man pleaded with terror-filled blue eyes.

"Lucy and Georgia, why don't you go relax outside by the pool -- it may get messy in here and you both look too lovely. Consider yourselves lucky you didn't end up with this cradle-robbing egomaniac," Margeaux said. The relieved young women gladly stood up on their long heels, click-clacked across the dance floor and departed into daylight.

"You, too, Willie. You're free to take the day off for a change. Go jump in the pool and relax. It's a beautiful sunny day on the Pacific," Margeaux said, tapping the dealer's shoulder and taking his spot behind the card table facing Balls.

"Thanks so much," Willie said, flashing a grateful but nervous smile before running for the door.

Howard looked like he was hoping for a reprieve, too, but Margeaux kept him waiting anxiously in his black chair under the lights.

Now it was just Margeaux and Balls all alone at the card table with cameras rolling and boom mics capturing sound. The naked girl remained silent for a moment, savoring this rare occasion when she was in control. She hadn't felt this good since she kicked Ventana's ass in Area 52. Now her mission target squirmed directly in front of her as he stared into the barrel of a gun once carried by a man paid to protect him. Balls snuck a few glances at Margeaux's bare breasts, a pathetic move even in this dark hour for the black king. *A sort of last meal for his eyes as his execution looms,* she mused.

Margeaux gathered the deck of black-backed cards with her left hand while she held the pistol with her right hand. She stacked the deck, bent it back with her left thumb and let the cards fall back to the table rapidly. The brief ripping sound cut through the heavy silence in the lounge. Then Margeaux's left hand fanned the 52 cards out face-down in a semicircle on the table between her and Balls. When she did that, Ballentine jumped in his swivel chair like he had just been zapped with the first jolt in an electrocution. His eyeballs popped open wide as he saw dozens of naked girls appear out of nowhere on the dance floor. They all looked exactly like the Margeaux in front of him. The only difference was they weren't pointing guns, but their eyes sure looked deadly as they glared at the trapped king.

"What's happening? Where did they all come from?" Balls shouted, pointing toward the dance floor.

"Who's they? What are you talking about?" the cameraman behind the bar asked.

"Don't you see all the naked girls? Over there? Out on the dance floor?" wild-eyed Balls persisted in a panicky voice while pointing wildly.

"No, I don't," the cameraman said, shaking his head.

"Howard? You see them, don't you?" Balls pleaded.

"Sorry king, but I don't see them," Nelson said, biting his lip while witnessing the feeble final moments of Robert Ballentine.

Margeaux let Balls sweat for a few seconds more as he gazed at 51 shadowy figures looking back at him, teasing him, mocking him.

"I remember reading somewhere that if you see a doppelganger it is a sign of misfortune or impending death," Margeaux said, gripping the gun tightly, raising it and pointing it at Ballentine's pony-tailed head now. "You see 52 of us in all -- that's an extremely grave foreshadowing for you. And obviously, queens -- not kings -- are wild today."

"Stop this madness and finish me off already!" Balls demanded as tears filled his eyes and hysteria took over.

"No! Someone else has volunteered to do that honor. There's a joker in every deck and she would like to have the last laugh. In this case it's the commander-in-chief of the United States of America. Madam President, please join this party!" Margeaux shouted toward the door at the far end of the dance floor.

The doppelgangers suddenly disappeared from Ballentine's vision and in walked 69-year-old President Margeaux Quigley. She wore a dazzling black-and-silver gown with modest black heels and, apparently, no longer required a wheelchair. She ambled slowly with no sign of a limp from her gunshot wound. When she approached the card table, she beamed with delight at the sight of Balls cornered and cowering for the whole world to see on his very own UKA network.

"Well, well, well -- I see the table has turned, King Balls," the president quipped with a laugh as she raised a black pistol at Ballentine's chest. "Checkmate, *mate*. This is for my fallen husband, my fallen colleagues, my stolen country and, yes, for me. Goodbye, Robert Ballentine!"

"No!" Balls screamed with two hands in front of his face.

President Quigley pumped Balls' chest full of bullets as he rocked backward in his chair with eyes of horror. He toppled over diagonally, twisted in agony and hit the black-and-white carpet face-down. Blood spurted out of the new holes in his tuxedo, through his nose and mouth, and pooled all around him. The time of death was 2:52 p.m.

Young Margeaux lowered her gun and set it gently on the card table. The president did the same.

At last. Mission accomplished, young Margeaux thought.

The cameras kept rolling as Margeaux walked around the table and hugged President Quigley for nearly a minute. They both cried tears of relief and joy.

"Now Miss Hero, maybe we can find you some clothes," the president said with a smile.

"You know, I would really love that," young Margeaux replied with a huge exhale.

"The Chinese have a lot of explaining to do, our military can get back to work rooting out the royal lords and death squads, and we've got a country to get back to," President Quigley said.

Young Margeaux pulled back from the president, placed her hands on her shoulders and smiled.

"I'm pretty good at dealing with captains," she said. "I'll go make sure he steers the ship back toward Wake Island. At least that's a U.S. territory."

"Yes, I suppose that's a good place to regroup and find a ride home," President Quigley said.

Chapter 33

Date: May 23, 2036
Place: Washington, D.C.

As Bill Cyr had predicted, once Robert Ballentine ceased to exist, the entire hostile takeover collapsed very quickly.

The Chinese leadership, as it said it would do, called Ballentine a home-grown U.S. terrorist who paid North Korean mercenaries to do the dirty work. Though it was harshly condemned by the U.S. and its major allies, China refused to admit it had been paid a huge sum to recruit North Korea, help coordinate the coup and covertly support it with military and technological aid.

With the president safe and the U.S. military able to fully flex its muscle again, all 49 of Ballentine's royal lords and every member of the Black Death was either killed or captured by the second week of April. The prisoners would be brought before military tribunals in the coming months. On top of that, a total of 27 turncoats within the U.S. government and military were arrested, charged with treason and awaited trials that almost certainly would result in the death penalty.

Despite the ongoing tensions with China and North Korea, President Quigley promised to focus her energy on looking inward and using the incident as a valuable lesson. America needed to get her own house in order: reduce her military presence overseas; channel more resources to paying down debts; shore up her inner defenses; root out potential traitors; and vastly overhaul an education system that was failing its children and leaving the U.S. frighteningly vulnerable to smarter enemies.

On a lighter note, young Margeaux Quigley had become a hero and instant sex symbol to the restored United States of America, which once again included Hawaii. The teen, who was now living at the White House and finishing her senior year of high school in Virginia, vowed to never show her naked body again on live TV, much to the disappointment of every teenage boy and hot-blooded male in the U.S. and beyond. Unfortunately for her, most of her ardent fans already had her memorable performance in Ballentine's queen contest finale preserved forever on their DVRs.

Young Margeaux's public relations team of Baker & Baker (yes, Jimmy Baker-17 and Jimmy Baker-69) came up with the idea of T-shirts that promoted both her and the president's acts of valor at the same time. On the white shirt's front, black letters read: "Who shot Balls?" above a photo of President Quigley and her raised gun -- a screen grab from the live TV shooting. Below the photo, in red letters, it said, "President Margeaux Quigley, commander-in-chief and savior of the USA." On the back, there was a large photo of young Margeaux Quigley in her blue senior prom dress and gold tiara. Underneath the photo, in red letters, it said: "America's First Queen's Day -- May 23, 2036."

Yes, President Quigley had decided to honor young Margeaux with the ceremonial title of queen for risking her life to save the commander-in-chief and the nation from Robert Ballentine. But the two Quigleys also had a practical strategy in mind to take advantage of the special teen's massive popularity. Sure to be in even greater demand with her new royal role, young Margeaux would make special appearances throughout the country to raise money for both national debt reduction and college scholarship funds.

Queen Margeaux Quigley was to be crowned on her 18th birthday -- May 23, 2036 -- on a gorgeous morning in the White House rose garden. Wearing a long, cream-colored dress with her black hair flowing down her back, young Margeaux carried a bouquet of roses in her left hand as she waved to her family, friends, White House staffers, media and a select group of citizens who were allowed in for the televised ceremony. A much bigger party, complete with music and fireworks, was scheduled for that night on the National Mall. Hundreds of thousands of people already were camped out between the Washington Monument and Lincoln Memorial in anticipation of the inaugural Queen's Night festivities.

Margeaux's mother and brother were among those smiling back at her as she waited to be crowned. Margeaux and the president already had begun planning to throw their mother a 90th birthday party in August at the White House.

Bill Cyr, Lou Ventana and G52 also attended the queen's coronation. Cyr was now working alongside his stepmother as a security aide at the White House. Ventana, still struggling from the effects of the CAR trips, had retired from the Navy and was taking some time off to write a book about his adventures. And G52, at the urging of young Margeaux, was revealed to the nation shortly after the country was restored to order in April. Margeaux believed the government should not be allowed to keep such secrets from its taxpaying citizens. They deserved to know if an alien life form had crashed into the Pacific Ocean and been retrieved by Navy Seals.

In late August, Queen Margeaux, Cyr and G52 would embark on an educational tour to coincide with the teen's fundraising efforts. The trio planned to "show and tell" for kids at more than 120 schools in all 50 states. Margeaux told G52 it was a good way to repent for his role in the deaths of the five boys at Kingsbury High School. Also, she insisted that from now on G52 and Cyr would only teach kids how to play chess the old-fashioned way -- on a flat board. They both agreed and Margeaux was eager for that new adventure to begin. College and a return to the soccer pitch would have to wait until the fall of 2037, Margeaux said. She needed at least a year to regroup from her ordeal and adapt to being queen.

President Quigley, meanwhile, had a re-election campaign to think about, but her poll numbers were looking stellar ever since the nation watched her blow away Robert Ballentine on live TV. On this beautiful May morning, however, the president wasn't worried about politics. She was just happy to be alive, free again and extremely thankful for the heroic efforts of young Margeaux on the high seas. She shed a tear and beamed with pride as she gently placed the gleaming, seven-pointed, diamond-encrusted crown atop the birthday girl's head. After warmly embracing the new queen and whispering in her ear for nearly a minute, the president motioned for her to say a few words at the podium, which was set up in front of the media and spectators. The small crowd cheered as she smiled, waved and walked gracefully toward the podium.

When the queen stood before the microphone, everybody went silent. Only the joyful spring sounds of birds singing could be heard. Queen Margeaux took it all in as she surveyed the amazing scene in front of her -- so many friendly, hopeful faces surrounded by fragrant blossoms bursting forth in reds, pinks and whites. It was also wonderful to see the dazzling red, white and blue of Old Glory rippling in the breeze above her. The solid black flag of Robert Ballentine turned out to be only a brief nightmare in the grand scheme of things. *I have my whole life still in front of me and so does America, she thought. Let's make the most of it, starting today.*

That's when Queen Margeaux leaned closer to the microphone and spoke from her heart: "Good morning to you all on such a beautiful spring day. I am humbled and honored to be crowned the first queen of the United States of America," she said to a rousing ovation that lasted for nearly two minutes. She blushed, grinned and blew kisses. "While all you've heard about me is true -- that I am from a different time, 1984 to be exact -- I still come from the same great nation as all of you. I will dedicate the rest of my life to making sure this country is the best she can be for all of her people."

Thunderous applause filled young Margeaux with joy. She had tears in her brilliant blue eyes as she continued, but she spoke clearly: "Before we run off to celebrate tonight, I want to leave you with one thought to reflect on. The Secret Service has been letting me drive to school like a normal person at least once a week. The other day, I was waiting at a red light and I noticed a bumper sticker on the car in front of me. I was struck by what it said and I think you will be, too. Apparently different versions of this same quote have been attributed to everyone from Jimi Hendrix of America, to Sri Chinmoy Ghose of India, to William Gladstone of England. Maybe that's because these words should ring true for every human being, every nation on this planet and every creature in the universe. The bumper sticker said: 'When the power of love is greater than the love of power, then we will know peace.' Let's become a nation of powerful lovers! Thank you fellow Americans for all of your love and support, and God bless you all."

The spectators erupted again and Queen Margeaux blew more kisses to her people. She carried herself with the elegance and poise of someone far beyond her 18 years. The president clapped with tears in her eyes. Even Lou Ventana applauded her leadership. Seconds later, the crowd began chanting, "God save the queen, God save the queen."

Later that evening, hundreds of thousands of Americans -- many wearing the T-shirts designed by Baker & Baker -- took up that same refrain between the Washington Monument and Lincoln Memorial. Fireworks exploded on high and dazzled onlookers with a brilliant array of colors against the black sky. The Reflecting Pool on the National Mall glowed and shimmered from the lights overhead. Soon, people began jumping into the water and dancing around as patriotic music blared from massive speakers. But nothing could drown out the united chorus of "God save the queen."

It surely was a wild scene.

###

About the author:
Jack Chaucer lives in Litchfield, Conn.,
with his wife and twin toddlers.

A special preview of the first chapter from his
second novel, **"Streaks of Blue:
How the Angels of Newtown Inspired One Girl
to Save Her School,"** follows this page.

Connect with Jack Chaucer online:
Twitter: @JackChaucer
Blog: http://www.queensarewild.wordpress.com
Goodreads:
http://www.goodreads.com/user/show/10499865-
jack-chaucer

Special Preview

Streaks of Blue:
How the Angels of Newtown Inspired
One Girl to Save Her School

This novel is written in memory of the 20 children
and six women who went to Sandy Hook
Elementary School in Newtown, Conn., on Dec. 14,
2012, and never came home.

Chapter 1 – Lakes of the Clouds

Nicole Janicek beamed, her glowing face a
lighthouse beacon for the sea of silent, stony
summits surrounding her in the late summer
twilight. Undistracted by the long, fine strands of
light brown and dyed-blue hair whipping around her
in the gusty mountain air, the teenager's spritely
blue eyes danced from peak to peak as they faded
into silhouettes. The moment itself was a fully
conceived poem, but Nicole was too consumed by
the blackening White Mountains to bend down,
reach into her pack and pull out her journal.

Then she heard her best friend's boot steps traversing the rocks to her left.

"The hut is filling up," Candace Cooper informed her as she approached, "but at least they have a decent bathroom. Wow, it's getting dark fast up here."

"And cold," Nicole added. "Hug me already, C.C."

Candace leaped over both of their packs and landed on Nicole's rocky perch. The soon-to-be high school seniors embraced warmly beside alpine flowers and a glassy blue pond -- one of several tarns on the beautiful broad shoulder of Mount Washington. The Lakes of the Clouds, as they are known, sit at about 5,000 feet between the summits of Mount Monroe (5,200 feet) and Mount Washington, the highest peak in New Hampshire's Presidential Range at 6,288 feet.

"Look," Nicole said, pointing to the purple northeastern sky. "Venus."

"Yes, the goddess of love," Candace said, her long, auburn hair pulled back into a ponytail as the wind buffeted them again. "I saw a few young men in the hut who could help keep us warm tonight and perhaps Venus is our sign."

Nicole gasped and pulled back from her slightly taller friend in semi-mock outrage.

"Don't even think about chickening out on me now, Candace," she said.

"They're going to catch us, Nikki. You know the rules -- no camping above the tree line. They can almost hit us with a stone from the hut," Candace replied, her green eyes pleading for a wooden roof instead of a nylon tent at such an exposed position. Despite the mercifully clear and hospitable conditions on this 55-degree night, the wind made it feel much colder and the girls weren't used to it after a long, hot summer.

"So what. I came here to sleep under the stars and that's what I'm going to do," Nicole said, her hands on her hips. "Are you with me or not?"

Candace gazed up and found more planets and stars shining back at her.

"God, they should call this place Lakes of the Cloudless tonight," she finally said. "If it weren't so damn clear, I wouldn't, but ..."

"Good, then let's hunker down and very quietly start setting up the tent ... like almost in slow motion," Nicole said, bending down and reaching for the folded up tent inside her navy blue pack. "Every minute that it gets darker and they don't see us works in our favor."

"OK, but I'm blaming it all on you if they catch us or a bear eats us," Candace quipped.

"I can live with that," Nicole said. "The bears live in the woods and we're above them here. Besides, some things are worth taking a risk for."

Dressed in a powder blue fleece, black wind pants and sand-colored hiking boots with red laces, Nicole took the lead in setting up the green nylon tent and spreading out a foldable cushion inside it for added support. They made camp on a stony patch of ground because they didn't want to risk getting in trouble for trampling the fragile alpine flowers. When Candace joined her friend inside the tent and stretched out her long, athletic body against the cushion, she immediately grimaced.

"Ouch, Nikki, this is most definitely gonna suck," she said, causing them both to laugh. "I really do hope we get caught now."

"Stop it," Nicole protested, punching her friend playfully in the shoulder. "We're roughing it for one night. That's all. It'll make you appreciate every other night when you have all the comforts of home."

"I swear I'm gonna start howling like a she-wolf until they find us and make us sleep in the hut," Candace threatened with a grin.

"Uh, no you won't, C.C. I'll tape your mouth shut."

"With what?"

"Duct tape."

"Duct tape? You brought duct tape?"

"Of course," Nicole said, tossing Candace a power bar from her pack as they now sat Indian style across from one another inside the cozy tent. "I also brought this," she added, grabbing a small head lamp and strapping the black band around her bi-colored hair so she could see as darkness descended on the ridge. "Cheryl used a head lamp just like it on her trek."

"You and your Strayed," Candace said.

"You should finish it," Nicole advised, referring to Cheryl Strayed's book, "Wild: From Lost to Found on the Pacific Crest Trail" (Knopf, 2012). "And you know she'd break the rules and make camp right here."

"I read enough of that book to know Cheryl would walk right over to that hut tonight and hook up with the first guy she met," Candace said, her mischievous grin returning.

"You make a valid point," Nicole said, nodding and taking a sip from her water bottle. "She was a real slut back in the day, but I do admire how honest she was about that in the book. I'm ..."

A flashlight suddenly shining against the tent made both girls flinch and freeze in place. Then they heard boot steps against a nearby rock.

"Oh shit, Nikki, I told you," Candace whispered, before smiling and adding, "I'm saved!" as she whimsically thanked a higher power with prayerful hands.

Nicole frowned, stuck out her tongue at Candace and then stuck her head out of the flap of the tent.

"Hello?" she said, squinting toward the flashlight.

"Hi, I'm Will from the hut crew," a handsome young man in his early 20s said as he squatted beside their tent with the flashlight on them.

Candace nudged Nicole aside and stuck her head out of the flap, too, causing Will to shuffle his squatted legs, lose his footing momentarily and nearly fall into the tarn. Clearly, he wasn't expected to see two teenage girls camping in this spot. Nicole and Candace both managed to stifle their laughter.

"Sorry to disturb you, ladies," Will said, quickly recovering and remembering why he was there. "But there's no camping permitted above the tree line or anywhere within a quarter mile of Lakes of the Clouds Hut. Do your parents know you're out here?"

"Yes," Nicole replied, her blue eyes defiant. "We may be young, but we're seasoned hikers. We're practicing to do the whole Appalachian Trail, maybe even the Pacific Crest Trail. We're not starting a fire and we're not trampling the flowers."

"Still, rules are rules," Will said with earnest hazel eyes and short brown hair. "We have a couple of bunks not filled at the hut so why don't you join us there. It's not far at all. "

Candace was attracted to the man and saw an opportunity to help her friend get Strayed in her way while possibly getting Strayed herself in an entirely different way.

"I'll make you a deal, Will," she said slyly. "I'll join you at the hut if you'll look the other way and let my friend Nikki here live out her dream of sleeping under the stars just this one time. How does that sound?"

The young man smiled and shook his head, but clearly he was entertaining the offer. When all of Candace emerged from the tent and she bent over to pull out her pack, Will just stared and had no words.

"You'd really do that for me?" Nicole asked Candace.

"Gladly," she replied, pulling her hair out of its ponytail and flipping it around in the wind for full effect.

"No fires, no ...," Will said, finally regaining his voice only to be cut off by Nicole.

"No trampling the flowers, got it," she said with a smile. "Thanks, the both of you ... I really mean that."

"I'll be back to check on you early, Nikki, or join us in the hut if you come to your senses. Otherwise, just call me if you need anything ... we do have working cell phones up here at least," Candace said.

"Anything else, mom?" Nicole asked as they began walking away.

"Yes, don't roll into the pond and drown," Candace yelled back.

"You be careful, too," Nicole shot back with a loaded smile that she hoped Candace saw in the glare of her head lamp.

When they were gone and it was certain she had been given the green light to camp under the stars 5,033 feet above sea level, Nicole climbed out of her tent and jumped for joy. She launched all 5-foot-6 of her toward the heavens and tried to grab a piece of the Milky Way as it cascaded above her. Though her boots crashed back onto the rocky ground, she felt her heart leap into space.

· · ·

Adam Upton surprised his younger brother when he suddenly veered the half-red, half-rusted pickup truck off the road and into the empty high school parking lot.

"What the hell are you doing?" Brody asked. "School doesn't start until next week."

Adam brought the truck to a screeching stop facing the large, open practice field on the left side of the sprawling brick school building.

"I'm about to give you your most important assignment for the school year," said Adam, who at 17 seemed nearly double the size of his 13-year-old brother. "And you're gonna do it when I tell you to do it because that's what freshmen are supposed to do -- kiss the asses of the upperclassmen."

"That's total bullshit," Brody protested.

Adam punched his brother in the left arm and laughed. Brody grabbed his arm in pain and hung his head. He was tired of being ordered around, overpowered and pummeled by his UFC-loving brother.

"Get used to it, son. Life is bullshit," Adam said with a nasty edge to his husky voice.

"You ain't my father," Brody said hesitantly, not looking at him and fully expecting another punch at any moment. "And whenever you start calling me 'son' something bad is about to happen."

Both boys had messy, wavy brown hair and brown eyes, but Adam was 6 feet tall, stocky and stubbly faced. Brody, whose growth spurt hadn't started yet, was only 5-4, fairly thin and didn't even sport peach fuzz on his cheeks yet.

"I'm the closest thing you got to a father, son ... Dad's so f----- up all the time. So you're gonna pull a prank for me sometime soon. Got it?" Adam said menacingly, his whole face boring into his brother, leaving no room for argument.

"OK, OK ... what the hell do you want me to do?" Brody asked, practically whining for mercy.

"You're gonna pull the school fire alarm for me," Adam said flatly, shifting his weight back toward the steering wheel.

"Why?" Brody asked after pondering the assignment for a moment.

"You'll see," Adam replied, his eyes now focused on the grassy field in front of the truck. "And if you're smart, you'll hide in the bathroom after you pull it. You really don't want to get caught up in a turkey shoot."

"What?" Brody asked, utterly confused.

"It's just a hunting expression, son," Adam said.

"Oh."

This novel is scheduled to be published in the fall of 2013.
Half of the proceeds will be donated to the Newtown Memorial Fund.

19499207R00135

Made in the USA
Charleston, SC
27 May 2013